Heat Deflectors and 99 Other Short Stories

Darryl Ponicsán

Heat Deflectors

Also by Darryl Ponicsán

The Last Detail
Cinderella Liberty
Last Flag Flying
The Accomplice
Goldengrove
Andoshen, PA
Tom Mix Died for Your Sins
The Ringmaster
An Unmarried Man
Eternal Sojourners
I Feel Bad About My Dick: Lamentations of Masculine Vanity and Lists of
Startling Pertinence

ISBN 978-1-960405-43-2
eBook ISBN 978-1-960405-44-9

Visit Darryl online—https://darrylponicsan.com
Cover design by Guy Corp—www.GrafixCorp.com
Cover illustration by Rick Geary—https://www.rickgeary.com/

STAIRWAY=PRESS
STAIRWAY PRESS—APACHE JUNCTION
www.StairwayPress.com
1000 West Apache Trail
Suite 126
Apache Junction, AZ 85120 USA

Dedication

To Cecilia

...only a dewdrop but within...tumult.
—author unknown

Foreword

WHEN I READ the title of Darryl Ponicsán's story collection I thought he was nuts. *Heat Deflectors and 99 Other Short Stories*...even with my poor math skills, that works out to 100 short stories. Most short story collections run 15-20 stories tops. Oh, so Ponicsán's are *very* short stories. So, he's even crazier, because it takes even more skill to write a very short story than a full-sized one. Miniature painters work harder than muralists. A friend of mine, flush with TV money, collects 17th century miniature paintings. Detailed portraits of British nobility, painted with a single human hair onto a thumbnail-sized piece of ivory. Take that, *Guernica*. So, I decided that maybe Ponicsán has taken an easy way out and written short stories that are more like introductions to fully realized work. Sketches of stories.

So, I started reading and it turns out I was wrong. These are not sketches. They are not fictional doodles. Rather, Ponicsán has created something unique and wonderful. He spotlights a defining moment in time—a brief glimpse into a character or a situation which deepens and deepens as the reader savors that moment. He created a narrative invitation to a more resonant reality, like snatches of conversations from the next booth of a diner which Ponicsán sifts through, choosing those that yield the most impact, the most insight.

Let's do a metaphor. Most photographs today are taken by high-speed cameras, where the photographer machine-guns dozens of images and goes back later and selects the best one. Before the invention of the motor-drive, photographers waited for the right moment...like the master of black and white candid photography Henri Cartier-Bresson who would wait all day for the right photo, what he called the "decisive moment," the instant that captured a scene or an individual, like a schoolboy caught with a knowing expression that gives a glimpse into his heart. The ultimate decisive moment was probably Robert Capa's photograph of a loyalist militiaman being killed during the Spanish Civil War with his head canted back and his rifle flying from his hands.

This is what Ponicsán does. This patience for the decisive moment, his ability to home in at a focal point of human experience for that which is honest and true…and Ponicsán manages this *100* times in this collection.

This is microdosing fiction, a stripped-down minimalism that demands attention.

Rolling into Reno on a Greyhound bus for the first time, you might think, this is where the desperate go to kill themselves. And you wouldn't be wrong.

How do you stop reading after that opening line to *Ceci N'est Pas Une Pipe*? How can you not be curious about who thought that about Reno and who agreed with that thought? Ponicsán doesn't wrap things with a tidy bow, he supplies no answers; he's more interested in crafting fishhooks than catching fish.

Many of the stories seem almost random, but they're carefully chosen and refined, the dialogue the soundtrack of everyday life:

- A woman offering her dead husband's shoes to a couple of his friends.

- A Triple-A pitcher worried about losing his fastball while having anonymous sex with a woman who nods reassuringly.

- A wife who doesn't drink but accompanies her drunkard husband to bars.

- A lonely old woman who goes to the airport to watch the luggage revolve around the carousel…and sometimes takes a bag home, excited at the idea of being caught and then opening the bag, sifting through the clothes, imaging their owners' histories, like Leakey at the Olduvai Gorge.

- Love stories, some bleak, some surprising: a French girl met by chance in Paris by a sailor on leave, making slow, sultry love in the steamy dimness of her flat, and when he gets up for a moment she says, "linger longer," and he thinks it's the most beautiful thing he ever heard. And he's right. The glory of chance, the futility of the present, a cascade of honesty.

Here's another example that reveals what Ponicsán's up to:

A man receives a text meant for someone else. A wrong number. A bitter text from an ex-lover, raging at his duplicity and cowardice for ending their affair.

There's a multiplicity of responses he can make to the mistaken text and all of them reveal who he is. He could ignore it, like most of us would. He could forward it to friends. He could respond cruelly, pretending to be the heartbreaker, winding the jilted lover up, mocking her for loving him. Instead, the protagonist assumes the identity of the heartbreaker and confesses his frailty and folly for ruining the relationship, telling her that she was the best thing that ever happened to him and that he wasn't worthy of her love. He sends the text to her, and we feel his inherent goodness, his desire to ameliorate the pain of a woman he will never meet, and then…she texts him back.

That's the end of the story and the beginning of something even greater that plays out in the reader's head and I hope to God something good comes out of it, I hope they meet for coffee, and I hope she's taken with him and the kindness of this stranger, and I hope he sees beyond her wounds and sees the possibilities. I want a happy-ever-after ending but I have no idea what Ponicsán wants. Ponicsán created an open dialogue and there's no telling where it goes. Perhaps the jilted lover is outraged at this invasion of her life and her privacy, perhaps she accuses him of playing off her vulnerability…perhaps the kind stranger understands why she was dumped. Hard not to wonder, and once again the reader is an integral part of the fiction.

Reflecting Ponicsán's own history, several of the stories are from the POV of sailors and the whole collection feels like ships passing in the night…time is short in these stories, or over or just beginning, but it's best to grab on and wave goodbye to a shadow glimpsed on the other ship, and maybe they wave back, and maybe they don't, but when that moment's over, it's over, never to be revisited again.

Ponicsán doesn't tell us stories, not in the traditional sense. He gives us a dynamic framework, a carefully chosen skein of moments, a strobe that illuminates for an instant and then is gone. The results are revelatory because we, the readers, are part of the process…and what do you bring to the table, pal? You need a seven-course dinner to feel satisfied? Tough. Ponicsán's working-class flavors explode in the brain like those petite bouche dollops of rarefied flavor that foodies are always going on about while we are thinking about the delights of a bacon cheeseburger.

Check how the whole of a marriage is contained in the first three lines of *Laughter in the Dark:*

"I do not hate everybody," Owen said in his own defense.

"Then it's not you, it's me," said his wife, June, in that passive-aggressive tone for which he had no appreciation.

"Sweetheart, there is a great difference between not liking anybody and hating everybody," he said in that condescending way that made her want to scream.

Edward Albee wrote a whole play, *Who's Afraid of Virginia Wolf* about a married couple like this, and it didn't have the propulsive heart, the tearful insight, the dynamic compression, that *Laughter in the Dark* does.

You'll be tempted to race through these stories but slow down, pilgrim, get to know the people and enjoy the ride through Reno….

—Robert Ferrigno

With 11 New York Times bestsellers, Edgar Award nominee Robert Ferrigno writes crime novels and speculative fiction including *The Horse Latitudes* and the *Sins of the Assassin* trilogy.

His colorful resume includes stints as a college professor, newspaper editor and reporter, professional poker player and video game storyline writer for Amazon and Microsoft.

He holds college degrees in philosophy, film-making and creative writing.

1

Heat Deflectors

THE PARKING LOT at the Camelot does not offer much shade. The palm trees provide a little, but the fonds can fall on your car with hardly any wind at all. That Saturday afternoon it was 118 degrees with a light breeze which made Lily feel she was in a convection oven. The singeing heat was her reason for going to the movies in the first place.

She pulled into the lot and scoped out a space under a lonely Chitalpa tree. A stroke of luck. She accelerated to the end of the lot, made two left turns and arrived in time to see a man in an old Mercedes take the parking place.

She lowered her forehead to the steering wheel and pushed back tears. When she raised her head, she saw the man walking toward her from his sad sedan. She hoped she wasn't in for any road rage; he got the shady spot after all. If anyone should be in a rage, it was her turn.

The man gestured for her to lower the window, and she did, though she worried that might be a mistake.

"I'm sorry," he said. "Were you going for that spot?"

"I was, but…"

"Please, I can move. Stay right here and I'll back out."

Was this one of those random acts of kindness she'd heard of but never experienced herself? She became aware of her flimsy tank top, which she wore without a bra because of the desert heat. The man backed out as promised and parked in a nearby sun drenched spot. She pulled into the shady space and saw him in her rear-view mirror setting up his windshield heat deflectors. She put hers in place, too, and they found themselves walking toward the theater side by side. She did not welcome having a stranger so close to her but under the circumstance could hardly turn away.

"Thank you," she said, "for doing that. I can't bear getting into a hot car."

"Women are like that," he said.

What an odd thing to say. She didn't know that all women were like that, how could he? Who wouldn't hate the seat burning your legs and searing through your shorts and panties and your hands burning when you touched the wheel. Hating all that did not have to be a feminine characteristic, except for the panties part, and this was Palm Springs after all, so who knew? He appeared straight, but she'd been wrong before. It didn't matter. He was not age appropriate.

The Camelot is a boutique triplex that as a rule devotes one screen to a film no one ever heard about. Tickets are sold over the concession counter. She asked for one for "Infinitely Polar Bear" and ordered a diet Coke. The man, still standing next to her, asked for the same thing.

"I guess we have similar tastes," he said.

God! She appreciated the shady parking space, but all she was interested in was a movie and a cool place to sit. Did he not realize he was making her uncomfortable? She made no answer but moved away from him and into the theater.

She sat one seat in from the aisle, which was her custom, meant to discourage anyone from sitting next to her, and if someone should it made it easier to change her seat.

He appeared at her side and said, "May I?"

She hesitated. Empty seats were all over the place. He may

have believed he was no longer a stranger. He added, "I live alone, so going to the movies…" He didn't finish the sentence, probably assuming, correctly, that he did not have to. How could she object? Still, she was not at ease with this imposed intimacy. How could he fail to see the nonverbal clues?

"Thanks. My name is Owen, by the way," he said.

Lily said her name was Christine.

She wondered if he had changed his mind the instant he heard what movie she was going to see. That would give him a reasonable excuse to sit next to her and chat her up, exactly as he was doing. He had probably planned to see the one about the Beach Boys. It would have been more his era.

"I've been looking forward to seeing this," he said, as though he had read her mind and wanted to put it at ease.

"Me too. My boyfriend is bipolar, so…" she said, explaining her choice of films, though in truth she didn't care what she saw. She wanted to get out of the apartment.

"Really? Hmmm. I enjoy watching Mark Ruffalo act. He seems genuine."

Probably gay. She *hoped*. She hated it when older men hit on her. Why do they do that? What makes them think she'd be interested?

He took a long draw on his diet Coke and said, "I imagine it's difficult to be in love with someone bipolar."

"It isn't easy. Can't leave, can't stay. Sympathy and fury. It's stressful, to say the least."

She went on to tell him, in the moments before the lights went down, some of what it was like to stand by a man who might at one moment be charming and bright and at another be lying in the fetal position. He nodded and listened without interruption, which was good, but she was relieved when the show finally started.

The film overwhelmed her and during the end credits she bent forward and cried silently into cupped hands. Who knows what this dude hoped for when he gave up his shady spot to a young woman wearing a minimum of clothing? *This* is what he gets. Enjoy.

He gently patted her back on the space between her shoulders. She flinched, shocked by this blatant invasion of her personal space, his bare hand on her skin. It was an assault.

"You have nothing to feel bad about," he said in a comforting voice, like a helpful teacher maybe. "I'm sure you're doing your best. He's lucky to have you. What's his name, your boyfriend?"

She couldn't answer. She kept her face in her hands. She should not have come to this movie.

He seemed to understand and said some more comforting words in his calm way until she stopped crying. "Well…" he said and got to his feet. "Take it easy on yourself." She fought the impulse to grab his arm. "Thanks for the company. I hope things work out for you. Try to stay cool."

She turned and watched him walk up the aisle to the exit.

His car was gone by the time she got to hers. She had lingered in the empty theater. She needed time to pull herself together. Her last boyfriend, Jamal, who was as well-adjusted as any she'd ever had, accused her of being a drama queen, creating crisis where none existed.

But it's all around you, isn't it?

2

Geranium

THOUGH SOME THINGS become lost in the folds of memory—the name of a classmate once loved from afar, a short term furnished apartment, a healed injury—abandonment can never be forgotten.

Their mother read to the three children the note their father left taped to the water heater only moments after she had read it to herself.

She was as abandoned as the children, more so since she knew him longer and in different ways. The note was in Spanish. She translated it as though it were the first clue in a scavenger hunt. "Look, Docia," she said, "this is your name, and Roberto, yours, too. Here's yours, Alfonso. Look where your father wrote down all of your names."

The water heater grumbled. Within a few weeks it would be gone, too, broken beyond repair, and shortly after that they would all be gone from that rented house in Chino, California. Until picking season began, they lived in a 1942 DeSoto, considered a luxurious mode of transportation in its day.

The abandoned family followed the harvest from one migrant camp to the next. Their mother carried with her a geranium planted in a coffee can and would set it up lovingly in whatever space they were assigned. She made a home of wherever they had to be and was determined the children would always be presentable and would have some fun in their lives, the kind that did not require tickets.

She eventually landed a job behind a lunch counter and married a regular customer, a responsible but unkind man.

Now grown, the children cannot remember, if ever they knew, why their father left them, only the way their mother read the note he left taped to the water heater and the indestructible geranium that traveled with them.

3

Departures and Arrivals

SIMONE FREQUENTS THE airport, but only before and after holidays and on Mother's Day. She moves from one boarding area to the next and pretends to read a magazine. It would never occur to her that she was a voyeur, taking in genuine displays of emotion, watching people saying their good-byes and clutching each other. Some of them would hold onto a sleeve to the last moment.

International flights are the most wrenching. Going far away means being gone longer, maybe forever.

At the end of the day, Simone falls in with a stream of arriving passengers and walks with them to the baggage claim area. As the luggage goes round and around, she moves closer, and looks for a bag that will never appear. Then she shares in the happy sense that their travels will soon be over.

4

Splatter

THE ARTIST CALLED out to his wife, who was also an artist, some say more talented than he. He asked her to come into his studio. Casual observation confirms that two dentists can marry and together open a successful practice. Two teachers can marry and work well in the same school. Two actors often marry, only to divorce and marry other actors. But two painters, abstract expressionists, run a greater risk in matrimony.

When called, his wife came, accustomed to being his first and most adoring critic. On the floor lay a large raw canvas splattered with house paint. He held in his hand a stick from the garden, still dripping with white paint, his arms folded across his chest, his head down, studying his own work.

She quickly planned what she might say about this new technique and the result of it. As always, she thought, he will want to hear that it is good, right after he pretends that it is bad.

"Lee?" he asked

"Yes, Jackson?"

"Is this a painting?"

5

The Oyster

"OWEN, OWEN, OWEN..." June sighed, listening to her ex-husband's long delayed confession, laying bare a soul she was no longer interested in seeing. They sat on her porch, the house she got in the settlement.

"I'd only been to New York once before, when I was down and out. I had to sleep in a 42nd Street movie house. The show was Fellini's "8½." I woke up from a nightmare into what I thought was another nightmare. Okay...I screamed, but not all that long or all that loud. This usher kicked me out to the street, which turned out to be the third nightmare."

He was setting up the contrast. Years later, he stayed at the Plaza Hotel, on his publisher's tab. The hot young writer destined for great things.

"Living the dream," said June, flatly.

"To be honest, my dreams were small and I kept them to myself. All I ever wanted was to be published, to legitimately call myself an author."

"Anyone can have that, now. Remember Siswein, our dentist? He's an author now. So is Rachael. Remember her?"

"Right. So I'm staying at the Plaza, and at Random House they were calling me a young genius. They wanted to lock me into a two-book deal."

Owen's first novel, "Raven Run," three months and four days from publication, already had great wind behind it.

"They took me to lunch, my publisher and my editor. Her name was Janice. She was only twenty-four. A NYU grad. Beautiful the way young intellectual women are hardly aware of."

The lunch went well. When Owen brought it up in conversation that he loved raw oysters, the publisher told the young editor to take their new genius out that evening for the best New York has to offer.

"It's not the oyster itself that's erotic, just looking at it," he told June, "it's the consumption of it. Eating raw oysters is like slurping wet skin. We had martinis first, then ordered two dozen oysters on the half shell. I downed more than my share, all the while looking at her right ear lobe. She had short hair, boyish, no earrings. No jewelry at all. We ordered two dozen more, with cold Chablis. I rambled on about what I was after in my writing, as though I knew. Human redemption, I thought. I know, it sounds precious now. She asked me about my favorite living authors. And then told me their sales figures! I was shocked that they were so low. A little depressed even. Half of them were kept on the publisher's list for prestige alone. Everybody talked about their books but nobody ever read them. I told her about you and kids back in California. She found it quaint and a little boring, excuse me, a lifestyle she did not see in her own future. I held an oyster aloft on its half shell, like a demonstration."

The martini had had its effect. Owen announced to the young editor that, "One of these could kill you."

She said, "Not here."

"Get the wrong one, not here but somewhere, get the oyster and..."

"Do we care?"

"Not a bit. Not a bite."

June said flatly, "She sounds just wonderful."

Owen and Janice walked together up Fifth Avenue, against

the current, toward the Plaza. He told her he didn't want the night to end. She didn't respond.

"I'd ask you back to my room, but..."

"I wouldn't mind."

That was the point in his story that June sighed, "Owen, Owen, Owen..."

"I expected her to turn me down, so I heard only the word 'wouldn't' and I was quick to give her an easy out. I started back-pedaling and apologizing before I realized she'd said yes."

Owen signed the two-book deal and in his new success looked for any excuse to go to New York. Occasionally she would come to Los Angeles. She was of another generation and was up for anything.

One night, in her bungalow at the Beverly Hills Hotel, she cried out that she loved him. He looked up from her belly and said, "You want to think that over?"

"No, I really do." She held his head. "I love you. So what?"

"She knew we had no future."

June asked, "Why are you telling me all of this now?"

"You deserved better from me, not a betrayal like that."

"Did you tell her you loved her, too? Because you never said it without the 'too'."

"No, I didn't say it. I kind of did, a little, but it was stupid, kind of, like, where were we?"

"Are you finished?"

"Yeah."

"Did you think I would want to hear that story?"

"No, but I needed to tell you."

"Then it's off your chest."

"I'm sorry."

"Are you, though?"

"Why wouldn't I be? Look at me."

6

Our Thing

AFTER DINNER THE two young married couples talked about the earliest event in life that each could recall. This was prompted by an article one of them had read in The New York Times.

The host surprised the others and even himself by how far back he could reach into memory. He could remember when he first wanted to match words to the things around him. He recalled pointing at a hassock in the living room and asking his mother, "What's that?"

He was not quite two at the time and could not be certain he had even those two words. Maybe he just pointed and grunted or cooed.

"That's ours," his mother told him.

Her answer did not satisfy his baby curiosity.

He pointed to a porcelain figurine on a shelf. His mother was fond of porcelain figurines.

"All of those are ours," she said. He pointed to the venetian blinds, and she said, "That's ours, too."

Could three such different objects all be identified by the same word? Ours?

That pattern of miscommunication between him and his mother continued for a lifetime.

After the guests went home, he and his wife loaded the dishwasher and went upstairs. He walked from the shower into the bedroom, naked and still wet. His wife was lying in bed.

She looked up at him, rolled her eyes, and said, "What is that?"

"That's ours," he said.

7

Salvage

BACK THEN IN that little town where Frank was born and raised, people had to take their own trash to the dump, which was an open pit two miles beyond the American Legion.

You backed up to a steep drop-off and overturned your trash cans into the pit. Frank had to go with the old man every Saturday, as a chore, but he enjoyed the weekly outing.

He was twelve when this happened, back when they were still calling every homeless encampment "Hooverville."

One day two hoboes, as they were called then, were scavenging at the dump, dressed in castaway clothes. One held a rope, the other was half-way down the pit, with the end of the rope wrapped around his waist. He held a big piece of canvas fashioned into a bag and searched for anything of value.

The hobo on top asked the old man, "Mister, okay if we go through your garbage before you dump it down?"

"Sure," said Frank's father.

That hobo then pulled his partner to the top. Standing off to one side, Frank and his father waited as they sorted through their refuse.

Frank said, "Jeez...yuk" and made a face.

His father looked down at him and Frank was struck by the disappointment in his eyes. He said, "It's an honest living, son."

8

Gemini

MURIEL FOUND THAT same boy walking across the quad and yelled, "Hey, you!"

He looped an index finger back at himself, mouthing, "Who, me?"

"Yes, you." She marched toward him with the assertive flair of a third-year theatre arts major. "You stood me up last night. And I never wanted to date you in the first place."

He had been asking her out ever since she walked through his Frisbee game twelve days before. Annoying her, really, because he wasn't her type. He dressed like a twelve-year-old and seemed to live in a world of play. On the other hand, he was hot. She finally said, "I'll go out with you if we can go to the Dieberkorn exhibit."

Muriel could tell he had no idea who Dieberkorn was. When she told him, "My favorite of the Bay Area Figurative Group," he still looked clueless.

He said, "I had something funner in mind."

Muriel had long outgrown words like "funner."

"Take it or leave it," she said.

He took it, but then never showed. She waited on a bench next to one more tiresome girder sculpture until she was too angry to go inside alone.

Now the boy who stood her up stood silently and submitted to her tongue-lashing, waiting for her to run out of steam. When at last she took a breath, he said, "Listen, what happened, and I'm sorry about that, is that you met my brother Jamal. We're twins, but we only look alike. He's the airhead. He's totally self-centered and you can't count on him for anything. I apologize for his behavior. Not the first time."

Stunned and somewhat embarrassed, she looked him over. He wore a Façonnable shirt, open, over an insignia-free T-shirt, clean Levis, and actual shoes. He appeared to be a grown-up. Also, every bit as hot as the airhead brother.

That same day, after getting to know each other over raspberry smoothies, for which he insisted on paying, they made love in her dormitory room. He was caring and tender, and she was turned on by the perversity of it—swapping one brother for another.

Jamal lay close to her for a long while, petting her and planning how he could keep this from unraveling. If only he had remembered to meet her at the gallery. He couldn't remember what he did instead.

9

Baggage

SIMONE WATCHES YOUNG mothers and fathers struggle to keep their kids off the luggage carousels. Skycaps push old people in wheelchairs, turning sharply to avoid collisions.

A heavy man rushes in from the concourse and scans the mob. He calls out frantically, "Margie, where are you? I'm parked illegally!"

Confusion and impatience are the norms down in the baggage claim area.

On impulse, she picks up a suitcase from the moving carousel. It's not heavy. A small red American Tourister, a weekend bag. She wheels it away as fast as she can move, like so many of the other travelers. She takes it to the short-term parking lot and puts it into the trunk of her Chevy Malibu.

Simone drives home feeling like a criminal, which in truth she has become. She imagines herself jet-lagged from some long journey, which might explain why she has someone else's suitcase in the trunk of her car. It looks like hers, she would have said. It was an honest mistake, or at least that's the way she would have constructed it, should she have been apprehended.

Back in her apartment, off LaBrea, she lays the suitcase on her bed, as she used to when she travelled. Her husband was the opposite. He would let a suitcase stand by the door and not unpack until the next day, if then. Simone always felt compelled to unpack the minute she got home. It was her way. They never traveled much anyway, and now that she is alone, she never leaves Los Angeles. The airport is as far as she gets.

She feels ashamed. Thievery, until now, was not among the inexplicable things she does. What if the owner had seen her and chased her down? She would have to give the owner his bag and return with him to the claim area. And then what?

The bag is not locked. Inside are a pair of khaki pants belonging to a tall man, two shirts, extra-large, and a plastic bag from a Portland hotel. His laundry is in the plastic bag: underwear, socks, and two black T-shirts. She uncovers a crushable hat, which she finds strange but does not know why. He might be bald and need to wear a hat in the sun, even if Portland doesn't get much sun, as she understands it. A toiletries kit is tucked under the laundry bag. It contains the usual things, plus three packaged condoms.

Simone had hoped to discover something mysterious about the owner of the luggage from its contents, to imagine his life and the reason for his trip. Disappointed, she unsnaps the ID cover, which reveals more about the owner than the contents did. His name is Darryl Jackson of Adams Boulevard, Los Angeles, not far from her own apartment.

She imagines a tall, voluntarily bald man, young, with a girlfriend in Portland, someone he sees only on weekends because he has to get back to work. They have safe sex, something that seldom enters her memories. She is guilt stricken to have Darryl's bag, doubly so because he must be Black, like her.

10

Man At His Best

NEIL HAS THE last three months of three different magazines in his one-chair barbershop, including that one which advises young men on how to be at their best. Wearing $900 shoes is basic. The same magazine lists the 100 best bars in America and the thing to drink in each of them.

This is the article up for debate while Gi-Gi is on the chair undergoing a tune-up on his style of choice: the "Pietro Pistole," inspired by the hero of the TV series "Peter Gunn."

The men in the barbershop consider themselves experts on the subject of bars, having grown up together in a culture of alcohol. They agree they would not be caught dead in any of those places described in the magazine; while admitting the likelihood they might be found dead in some other bar, as indeed one of them would be in the near future.

"In a good bar you should never be reminded that it might be daytime outside," says Eddie. "No windows looking out or people looking in."

Agreed. What else?

"No drink should ever have more than three things going into them," says Chewie.

"Except for a bloody Mary."

"And nobody should be allowed to order a bloody Mary

after one PM."

"No live music," says Joey.

"No jukebox either."

"And no food."

"Except for chips and pretzels," says Gi-Gi.

"Maybe a pickled egg."

"The bartender should be named Dave or Kathy."

"You lost me there. I don't see how that makes any difference."

"Would you be okay with a Jeffrey?"

"No, I don't think I would."

Their favorite bartenders were already named Dave and Kathy.

"What about televisions?"

"One on the game with the sound up."

"A place that calls you a cab and puts it on your tab."

"That's asking a lot."

"We're talking best here."

"No mirrors."

Gi-Gi says, "What are you, a vampire?"

"Who wants to look at himself with half a heat on?"

"Maybe one framed photograph on the wall."

"Like who?"

Neil and his three clients ponder this for a long moment. No one was willing to make a fool of himself by suggesting someone the others would think unworthy.

Eddie finally offers, "Rocky Marciano," and that nails it, a unanimous choice.

"Reasonable prices and intelligent conversation."

"Where everybody knows your name," says Gi-Gi.

"Even *I* don't know your name," says Chewie. "I know it ain't Gi-Gi."

The others laugh. His name is Eugene.

When the last of them has his haircut, they go next door to

the bowling alley for a drink.
  The one thing every bar should have?
  Proximity.

11

Ceci N'est Pas Une Pipe

ROLLING INTO RENO on a Greyhound bus for the first time, you might think, "This is where the desperate go to kill themselves." And you wouldn't be wrong.

Muriel, however, was far from desperate and did not go there for that purpose, or for any other reason really. She didn't *go* there at all in the way one thinks of it. She bounced out of Berkeley propelled by impulses of her own and landed in Reno.

A reasonable walk from the bus station and over the river is a joint called Peg's Glorified Ham and Eggs, where they put out a breakfast anyone might want to eat, at a fair price, and maybe that had something to do with Muriel's not getting back on the bus as it continued eastward.

What's more, July was just beginning. For the entire month Reno is all about art: theatre, music, painting, posing. Live events every day in the park, by the river, and on the streets.

Dada comes alive in Reno in July. Every kind of artist from chain saw sculptors to half-blind pointillists, middle-aged punk guitarists to schizoid collage makers, visionary cowboy poets to Jack Mormon surrealist painters, as an ad hoc group take over some low rent motels, move out the furniture and create pop-up studio/galleries. The art lover can wander from room to room, taking it all in. They call the movement "Nadadada," and it can get freaky.

Muriel had an iPhone—who doesn't?—and with it she put together a portfolio of found objects arranged in juxtapositions. She called them post-studio sculptures and gave them titles like, "The Passionate Tumult of a Clinging Hope." She composed a *vita* that included an imaginary MFA from Toronto and an impressive number of individual shows in fictitious galleries in New York, Philadelphia, and Munich. She added an arcane artist's statement of her spirit and intentions and submitted it all to a jury. Called for an interview, she charmed them into giving her a riverside loft subsidized by the city for juried artists.

Reno has more artists per capita than Paris. Marcel Duchamp turned them all loose when he said that art is what the artist says is art. No bad art exists, and for that matter no good art either, only art that succeeds or fails at what art is supposed to do, and nobody knows what art is supposed to do.

Muriel comes close.

12

Laughter in the Dark

"I DO NOT hate everybody," Owen said in his own defense.

"Then it's not you, it's me," said his wife, June, in that passive-aggressive tone for which he had no appreciation.

"Sweetheart, there is a great difference between not liking anybody and hating everybody," he said in that condescending way that made her want to scream. "I thought you might find it funny. Excuse me for treating you like a friend."

"You don't *have* any friends! What you find funny other people see as twisted."

"Thank you, Doctor Phil."

"Not funny."

"Funny as hell," said Owen.

This conversation started over the caucuses in Iowa, in which they found some common ground in absurdity, but then it took a turn when he told her of his latest prank.

The caucus event in Iowa was so monumental that it burned all the oxygen allotted to a twenty-four-hour news cycle on cable TV. Owen sat in front of the nightly news and yelled at the screen, a drink on the armrest. June took it that he was furious, as well he might be, but she was misinterpreting yet again what he considered entertainment and his own audience participation.

"It reminds me of the Grammy Awards," he said.

"The Grammy Awards! It's nothing like the Grammy Awards."

"Professional wrestling, then."

"Kind of."

"But more like an awards show. Rubio, the boy in the bubble, thanks God and his Lord and Savior, Jesus Christ, like some gangsta rap artist. Cruz, who may be scarier even than Trump, also gives a shout-out to Jesus, without whom he would not be standing there. They fall short of blowing a kiss heavenward, but then winning a Grammy is a bigger deal than getting twenty-three percent of Iowa Republicans to caucus for you. Do they even know what 'caucus' means?"

Owen went on to create for June a scene in heaven: God and His Son on Lazy Boy recliners, having a beer, watching the returns, fist-pumping and yelling, "Yes!" every time one of them is thanked publicly.

"You shouldn't ridicule someone else's religion."

"Why not?"

"Because it's not right."

To change the subject, he let her in on his recent prank, characteristically a one-man operation with no observable payoff.

Owen was one of the volunteers who sorted books for the library sale. One day while thus engaged he leafed through a book by Oprah, "What I Know for Sure," to determine its genre. Self-help or memoir? He imagined some woman thrilled to find it. Wouldn't it be funny, if...he took out his fountain pen and in what he imagined Oprah's handwriting might look like, inscribed on the fly leaf, "To Gale— What I know for sure is that you are one royal bitch. Oprah."

"Gale is like Oprah's BFF," June objected.

"That's what makes it so funny."

Later in that same session of sorting books he inscribed a

John le Carré book with a cryptic message to a fellow spy. When he found a Bible at the bottom of a cardboard box, he wrote, "To Mother, Hope this makes more sense to you than it did to me. Your son, Jesus H. Christ."

"Not funny," June said.

"Humor can't be explained. You either get it or you don't."

"Then I don't."

Owen knew an immigrant named Hector who worked at a nearby convenience store. Hector spoke Spanish at a breakneck pace, but he spoke English even faster than Spanish. No one could understand him in either language. If Hector laughed while racing through a story, others would laugh, too, giving themselves up to it. You didn't need the words. Sometimes, though, middle of the night, he would get it and wake up June with his laughter in the dark.

13

Fair Warning

CHEWIE, ONE OF the band of veterans together since grade school, stepped up to the stage after the break. His eyes were watering. This was when dive bars were full of smoke. He picked up the guitar and lowered himself to his stool. He strummed a three-chord progression looking for some idea of where he would go with this. Mary Ellen, his faithless girlfriend, sat at a table with three others like her. He sang just over her head, mournfully slow, improvising the lyrics.

"Eddie misses bacon, and Neil misses booze.
Gi-Gi misses his brother, Joey misses Newport News.
Kathy misses 'Desperate Housewives.'
Davey says he misses the sea.
If you keep on doin' what you're doin',
You're gonna be missin' me."

14

Home

THE WOMAN WHO owned the apartment returned from her vacation in Barcelona. Rachel and Sophia took no notice. Frank asked, "Would it be all right if I left this larger suitcase for a few days?"

"Yes, of course, and thanks again for taking such good care of the girls."

"They were perfect French ladies."

"Well, technically, they're Siamese."

He walked to the taxi stand on Boulevard Beaumarchais and took a cab to de Gaulle.

Many years before, someone warned him not to go back to Atlantic City, a place of such good memories. It was the family's only vacation spot, and as a child he thought it a magical city. It was where he saw the ocean for the first time and was awe struck by its vastness. He can still remember the Steel Pier and a horse who dove into the water from a great height. He took his friend's advice and never returned. Other friends who had been there recently assured him that he had made the right choice. No one, however, warned him not to return to Malta. No one he knew had ever gone there.

It was a short flight from Paris, shorter than he thought.

He took a bus from the airport to Valetta, remembering

the hub where it would stop, at the gateway to the city, where the buses swarmed. The hub looked the same, bustling with young people, though some of them looked menacing to him now. After he got off the bus, he realized that the cranky driver had cheated him.

Frank strolled the short distance to the Hotel Phoenicia, a victory walk of sorts. When he was first in Malta as a sailor so many years before, he dreamed of staying in such a grand place.

Now once inside he saw it was less than grand.

The Green Lantern, an inviting English pub where he had met Mary and may have fallen in love had been turned into a pizza joint, currently shut down by the health department. The streets felt different, the people oddly indifferent. Since he had been there that time, Malta had become the most densely populated country in the world. It seemed joyless now.

He sat at the bar of a restaurant during a mid-afternoon lull and tried to talk to the owner, a sour-looking woman who was cleaning up. She showed no interest. He told her about spending ten days in Malta as a U.S. sailor and how much he loved his time there. The woman wasn't even alive then and she didn't love it now, she let him know.

"Why not? he asked.

Without hesitation she answered, "The North Africans."

Malta was the best step to the rest of Europe and desperate migrants risked their lives on unseaworthy crafts to get there, but he did not say anything about that to the unhappy lady preparing for the next cruise ship to disembark.

He wondered if Mary was still alive and how he might find her. If he ever knew her last name, he'd forgotten it, though she remained fresh in his memories.

What was the point of going to a place you loved fifty years before? It wouldn't be there in the same way. How did it matter to wonder about a girl who once made you dream. He felt blue and wanted only to go home. He was relieved after three lonely nights to board the plane back to Paris.

He checked into a little hotel in Place des Vosges for his last night in Paris. He took the long walk to retrieve his luggage and to give Sophia and Rachel a farewell pet.

"Thank you for letting me sit the cats."

"Thank you. Will you be going home now?"

"Yes, tomorrow."

He wandered down Boulevard Henry IV toward the river, pulling his suitcase behind him, like any other tourist in transit. His blues would not go away, so he let them in. He turned and stopped at brasserie Le Sully. He stood at the bar and ordered a pastis. The woman gave him his drink and a tiny plate of olives. She asked, "Were you away?"

He was touched that she asked. They had never talked before.

"I was. For just a few days."

"Bienvenue à la maison."

The question rose in his mind: was he already home?

15

Hand to Hand

FOR MOST SAILORS the Navy was one hitch and out, but cribbage goes on forever.

Every Wednesday three Navy veterans and an Army draftee got together in a booth at the Town Square to play the game on a board shaped like a woman's leg. They were all Vietnam War vets, but only of them had ever seen a shot fired in anger. That would be Eddie, who survived being shot himself. He had a Purple Heart in a drawer somewhere. He needed no reminder.

"I had this shipmate named Evans," said Joey. "Only eighteen, hay still in his hair."

They laid down cards and counted pegs. As he shuffled the cards, Eddie asked, "What about him?"

"He saw combat. Hand to hand."

"In the Navy?"

"I thought you said your ship was called the Chicken of the Sea?"

"It was. We avoided conflict, but Evans fell in love with an Italian whore named Gina."

"In Italy?" asked Gi-Gi.

"Yeah, Naples. That's how come she was Italian."

"Go on."

"Evans was a good Christian boy. He wore a crucifix on a

chain around his neck, along with his dog tags."

"You're allowed to do that."

"One night he gives the rig to his new love Gina, dog tags, chain, crucifix. No intel on what she gave him." The others laughed. "The next night Evans gets separated from the rest of us and he has to find his way back to the ship on his own. He's lost and alone in a deserted Naples alley, stinks to high heaven, and here comes trouble. A dago with a knife. Evans was scared, who wouldn't be, but what made him crazy when the mugger got closer was he was wearing Evans' crucifix rig that he gave to Gina as a gift of love. Had no doubt, so Evans jumped him first, sideways missing the blade, and he got a hand around the chain and his knee on the guy's back. The dago went down and Evans twisted the crucifix right into his throat, 'til the guy stopped breathing. He never saw Gina again. Kind of knew he wouldn't."

Joey laid down his cards.

"Fifteen two, fifteen four, there ain't no more. That's the only sailor I ever knew killed a gook in mortal combat."

16

4ever

Herewith, the entire text:

"Dayvid: U lost a friend 4ever. Bye bye u troll/tool. Bus left! Now u can do whtevr u want with whmevr. U were never a friend 2 me. A friend would have been there, so there u go. Teresa."

Owen had Teresa neither in his contacts nor in his memory. The Caller ID was a telephone number with the same area code as his, but he did not live in that city anymore. A misdial, obviously, but why was Dayvid not in Theresa's list of contacts? They seemed close enough to love and or hate each other. Teresa would never know that Dayvid did not get a well-deserved piece of her mind. Why did she even have to punch in a number, resulting in a misdial? Is it possible she used a friend's phone, but why would she, Owen wondered. Whtevr.

Owen weighed three options: ignore the message; inform Teresa of her mistake; or reply as Dayvid for his own amusement. He chose the last option. He always enjoyed a prank, especially one without a payoff beyond his own imagination.

Herewith, Owen's reply:

"Teresa: I am sorry for evrythng. U R right to call me a troll, but I will remember only the good things about U. U were always too good for me and will be much happier with me out of the picture. I will love you 4ever. Dayvid."

He considered the tone and content of his prank in light of what currently could and could not be said properly without losing a job or getting cancelled. Was it malicious? Not at all. The message itself was gracious and sympathetic. It might be what the heart-broken girl needed, closure, a bit of a victory even. Besides, Owen did not have a job to lose, and if possible, he was on the brink of cancelling himself.

That was the sum of the thought he gave to the whole episode.

Teresa, it should have been considered, now had options of her own. Like Owen she took the last one: she replied.

17

Linger Longer

AS A YOUNG PO3 aboard the USS MONROVIA Frank had the good fortune to be anchored for a week in Nice. He took five days shore leave and boarded a train north to Paris, where in Pigalle that first night, he met a French girl, a waif, who told him she was a typewriter *méchanicienne*. He had never thought of such an occupation.

"I am very clever with it because of my long thin fingers."

She held them up for his inspection.

Most of her was long and thin, and the rest a bit ragged. They met in a tabac, both of them fascinated with a new type of jukebox equipped with a TV screen that played videos set to the music but bearing little connection to the lyrics of the song.

She initiated the conversation in passable English and he filled in using what was left of two years of high school French. She did not live in Paris but had come from Lyon, asleep in the back of someone's car after an all-night party and unnoticed by the driver until he parked the car on rue Dante.

"I live in the night," she explained.

She had no money and no place to sleep and did not seem to care. They wandered the streets together, smoking his tax-free ship's store cigarettes, tiring out at dawn at Les Halles, the old Les Halles, the stomach of Paris, where they had steaming onion soup, a baguette, and cheap brandy. He invited her back to his two-star hotel room and they made an awkward, bilingual kind of love on the narrow bed hardly big enough for one of them.

Afterwards, when he turned in the bed as though he might leave it, she said in her disarming accent, "Linger longer."

He turned back and held her against him.

"I never heard two more beautiful words."

"True?"

"True. Say it again, in French."

"S'attarder plus longtemps."

"Not as good."

"Perhaps I speak English better than I think I do."

"Oui."

They spent all five days together, and then he had to return to his ship. He paid the hotel for an extra night so that she could plan her next move or to linger alone.

On the train back to Nice he thought about her long thin fingers with which she reached into the bowels of troubled typewriters.

Frank returned to Paris several times over the years and wound up living there, but he never saw her again, or anyone like her, or those fingers.

18

The Perfect Stranger

SHE WAS UNAPPROACHABLE, out of his league. Jamal had seen her at the Straight before, sitting with the same group of girls. Now she was alone, studying her notes and having a late lunch of salad. He came out of the line with a grilled cheese and bacon sandwich, his favorite. He sat across from her but down a couple spaces. No doubt she noticed him. There were plenty of other places to sit.

The letter that was addressed to him in ink, still sealed, was in his shoulder bag. He removed it and propped it against his Coke. He squeezed a small pile of mustard next to his sandwich. He stared forlornly at the letter as he had his lunch, and out of the corner of his eye he caught her glancing at him.

Her salad was disappearing. That she would stay there longer to study was not a sure bet. The Straight was not the quietest place on campus, and she might have a class to attend. Jamal took a deep breath and slid down the bench, holding the letter between two fingers like something he found in the mud.

"Excuse me," he said.

"Yes?"

"I have something here I don't know how to deal with," he said, referring to the letter.

"What is it?"

"A letter from my girlfriend...ex-girlfriend."

"And this is of interest to me why?"

"That's the point. I don't know you, you don't know me. I can't go to a friend, because...well, my friends weren't that thrilled with her to begin with. She dumped me, in a *text*, and then changed her status on Facebook. She said some terrible things that hurt. They still do. So now she's sent this letter, and I'm afraid she's unloaded a year of resentment on me. I want to burn it, but I just can't."

"Hmmm."

"Would you be cool with reading it? Please? Read it like something you found on the floor. You don't know anybody involved."

"I wouldn't read a letter I found on the floor. I would take it to lost and found, or a mailbox."

"Okay, if it feels like, too creepy, I can find someone else. It's just that somehow you look right, like the perfect stranger."

"I do?"

"I have a sense about people."

"Not about your girlfriend, apparently."

Jamal smiled. It was said by some to be his best feature, sardonic, maybe dangerous, but always disarming.

"If I read it, what then?" she asked.

"All you have to do is tell me whether or not *I* should read it."

"How would I know?"

"You'll know. I want to stay positive in my life. I wouldn't want something hateful to be my last memory of her. I'm going to let in only good thoughts from now on."

"That's what everybody says."

She held out her hand like a teacher waiting for that gum in your mouth. He gave her the letter. She cut one corner with an elegant fingernail and tore it open. He watched her read. Her face revealed nothing of what she might be reading.

Finally, she folded the letter and put it back into the envelope.

"Jamal..."

He was startled. "How do you know my name?"

She smiled. "It's on the envelope, and the letter starts with, 'Dear Jamal.'"

"Oh, right."

"Jamal, you don't want to read this letter."

"That bad, huh?"

"I'm afraid so."

"Well, thanks. That's all the closure I need. What's your name?"

"Sheila."

"Nice. Well, thanks, Sheila. I hope I haven't made you uncomfortable."

He got up to leave but she invited him to stay and asked if he'd like to split a sundae. She wanted one desperately but should not eat a whole one by herself.

As it turned out, she ate little of it. Jamal, on the other hand, acted like a child given a treat after a trauma. They talked about their respective situations at Cornell. Jamal was by then a grad student in computer science. She was doing a dissertation on methods of teaching the novel. They made a date to see whatever French film was showing that Saturday night.

"What shall I do with this?" she asked him as he walked away.

"Burn it."

Here is what the letter said:

"Dear Jamal, I'm too embarrassed to text or call, so I'm sending this snail mail. I don't know what came over me. Mood swings, I guess. You are the best thing that ever happened to me. You are the sweetest and gentlest and most loving man I've ever known and I hate myself for treating you so gross. Can you ever forgive me? Can we start all over, as though I never was such a bitch? I love you.

Your Gwen."

Jamal did not have to know what was in the letter. He wrote it. He wondered when Sheila would figure that out. If she hadn't already.

19

You People

WITH THE SUITCASE she stole beside her, Simone drives slowly, looking for the address on the ID tag.

The house on Adams is one of those large two-and-a-half-story homes that decades before became too much to maintain for the black families who owned them, and they turned them into rooming houses. Simone knocks on the door. It is answered by an obese woman who is used to opening the door to strangers.

"Good morning, I'm looking for Darryl Jackson."

"Well, you're in luck. He's right upstairs. I'll buzz him. Sit down here on the sofa and put your feet up. It's going to be hot today." She draws out the word "hot" to let Simone know how hot it's going to be.

Simone sits and rehearses again what she will say. He will have to believe it. What choice did he have?

She sees his feet first and then his legs coming down the open wide stairway. Seeing the man himself sets her back. Darryl Jackson is a white boy. She has been picturing a black man with a shaved head and a beard, and here is a clean-cut white boy looking like one of those Mormon missionaries, living on Adams Boulevard in a black rooming house.

"Darryl?"

"Yes, ma'am."

He looks as confused as she.

"I have your bag," she tells him and pulls it from the side of the sofa into view.

"Wow, that's fantastic! Thank you!"

"I picked it up yesterday by mistake, at the airport, and last night when I realized...well, I came right here."

"Thank you so much. It's a new bag."

"Just move here?"

"In May. I'm rooming with a friend from the Navy."

He must feel some need to explain himself, she thinks, and she is relieved.

"Do you have a job yet?"

Older women can get away with asking young men anything they want to.

"I do," he says. "I'm near the end of my training period. I'm a social worker for the county. Old Age Assistance."

"Oh, my."

"Is something wrong?"

"No, no, it's just that I was a social worker, too," she says. "Also for the county. Medical Aid to the Aged. Retired now."

"What a coincidence! Fantastic!"

Simon remains seated on the sofa, his bag at her feet. Things are fantastic to this white boy. And sometimes to her, but not in his way.

"Yes," she says. "Thirty years. I started as a transcriber, and worked my way through Cal State Fullerton, got my degree, and kept working in the same building, but as a social worker."

"Fantastic! You know what we called you people in the Navy?"

"You people?" she says, arching her spine involuntarily. This white boy isn't going to last long in South Central calling an old black woman "you people."

"Yes, enlisted guys who work their way up through the ranks? And become officers? We called them mustangs. I don't know why, it's just what they were called. So you're a mustang."

She smiles and says, "I'm Simone. Just Simone."

"Well, thank you, Simone, for delivering my bag."

"Simone, the mustang. You know, in my life I've been called worse."

20

Amsterdam

"KLM PASSENGERS MOHAMMED Abdula and Youssef Ubaidah on flight six-o-six to Amsterdam, please report immediately to gate A-Two. The doors will be closing shortly after this announcement."

The older couple heard the announcement for the second time, word for word.

"Who *does* that?" Harry asked his wife. "They're in the airport, probably been here for awhile, if they're flying to Amsterdam. What the hell?"

"They might be in the bar. You can't hear announcements there."

"What's a Mohammed doing in a bar?" Louise told him in a harsh whisper to lower his voice. "Anyway, they know when the flight is leaving, don't you think?"

"You don't know that the two of them are traveling together. You just assume that."

"Two people? Two separate individuals would be so out of it to miss a flight to Amsterdam? Who happen to be Muslims?"

"You don't know that either."

"That's true. I'm making a wild guess that Mohammed and Youssef aren't Lutherans."

"And that was a little racist, about the bar."

"What? Mohammeds are not supposed to drink. It's all they talk about, besides death to America."

"Keep your voice down."

"What am I saying?"

"Mohammed could be having a ginger ale. Or he could be non-practicing."

"The hell. Non-practicing?"

"Like us."

They were sitting in the more comfortable chairs, the ones in the middle of the international concourse. Alaska Air was using that terminal temporarily. Temporarily forever, it seemed. Their own flight to Palm Springs had been delayed forty-eight minutes, more or less the length of the flight itself.

"Forty-eight minutes," said Harry. "Who comes up with that? Who calculates it will be forty-eight minutes instead of forty-seven, because it never is what they say it's going to be."

A man in an orange vest walked by asking, "KLM passengers? Anyone going to Amsterdam?"

"Yeah, like they would be sitting here," said Harry, not to the man, who was only doing his job, but to Louise. "This has got to be upsetting for KLM personnel. Nobody likes to leave passengers behind."

"What about their luggage?"

"I think they have to offload it. There's another delay, if not a whole evacuation. You can't have luggage flying without a passenger to match it. Especially if it belongs to Mohammed and Youssef."

"Shhhh…"

"What am I saying?"

"It doesn't involve us."

"I'm just saying. We've been here for two hours. Are we going to wander off and forget we have a plane to board?"

"Maybe they don't speak English."

"They have watches, I'm sure."

"Maybe they're not like us."

"Well, yeah, I would guess they're not like us. For one thing, we'd be on that plane to Amsterdam."

The announcement was made again, louder, more urgently, and this time it was said that the doors would close in three minutes.

Louise had heard about Amsterdam, both the good and the bad. She wished she was on that plane.

21

Shaky the Cop

BACK THEN, IN that little coal mining town not far from Scranton, a cop's job was a political favor and required no more than a single afternoon of training. The police force officially numbered three, including Chief Sweeney, who sometimes doubled as dispatcher.

One night, Shaky was in his parked squad car, singing a Frankie Laine song. "To spend one night with you, in our old rendezvous…" Nobody knew why he was known as Shaky. His hand was steady enough. In the coal regions, however, a nickname in first grade would be yours for life, for better or worse.

He saw a new Packard go through a red light. It might have been amber. He called Chief Sweeney on his new two-way radio and connected with his teen-age son, who often spelled the chief.

After Shaky explained the situation, the kid told him to give the Packard a ticket if he wanted.

"Can I turn on the siren?"

"Better not. People are sleeping."

"What about the flasher, you?"

"Knock yourself out."

The Packard pulled over at the foot of Peddler's Hill, still inside the city limits. Shaky grabbed his citation book and walked to the driver, who rolled down his window. The driver was clean-shaven and well-dressed. His wife was prim. Their two children were both frightened and fascinated in the back seat.

"'Evening, officer."

Out of towners. No one from around there ever called him officer.

"You went through a light back there on Center Street."

"But it was amber."

"That's when you're supposed to use caution."

"I thought I did. You don't have to stop unless it's red, and there was no traffic anywhere."

"Say, are you tryin' to tell me my business."

"No, sir, but..."

"No buts."

It was becoming an interesting interrogation, "sir" and all that. Shaky thought he had the upper hand. He liked to catch miscreants in a lie.

"This looks like a brand-new car."

"It is. We're out putting some mileage on it."

"Looks dear."

"It's not cheap, but I got a good deal."

"Where youse from?"

"Pittsburgh. We're on a family driving vacation."

Bingo!

Shaky gave it a dramatic pause, then leaned toward the open window.

"If you're from Pittsburgh, like you say, how comes you got a Pennsylvania plate on this car."

The driver looked at his wife, whose expression told him what he already knew. They should have stayed on the turnpike.

22

Rehab

OWEN COMMITTED HIMSELF to a rehab of his own making for a self-inflicted addiction. He had bottomed out and now needed help. Why is it that some things happen too slowly and then so suddenly? Did it really have to be that way? Could he actually do without them? Did he have the power to finally kick it?

You see? Adverbs were wrecking him and he could not break the habit.

He tried writing without adverbs but like a spiteful stepchild fell back into abusing their use. As with many unfounded rebellions his addiction was self-destructive. He knew that. His women were rather beautiful, quite alluring or painfully shy. His men were truly brave, crudely direct, or stoically silent. And Owen? He abused adverbs unconsciously.

He was not the only one. In the current deluge of self-published books, produced without benefit of editors, no one with a basic knowledge of grammar was there to intervene. His own editor enabled his habit, allowing him to cry out adverbs in moments of passion. His few friends were willing readers but all they demanded was a good story. He doubted they ever paid attention to the dangerous lure of adverbs. Back when he was still being influenced by Hemingway, he shot down adverbs as soon as they insinuated themselves in his manuscripts. Then over time he fell off the wagon.

During the course of a Happy Hour at the Purple Room (which in the desert can last all day) he sat alone at a table with a Manhattan and one of his early novels. He went through the book he hadn't read since it was published and marked each and every adverb with a blue hi-lighter. Pausing to flip through the spotted pages, he was truly horrified and deeply ashamed. Did no one love him enough to intervene?

How could he have let this addiction spin out of control? When and why did he become a slave to "obliquely" and "archly" and "surreptitiously" and, oh, God, "*just*." "He just left." "She just finished." "The rain fell just in the foothills." Owen looked around the lounge to tell any lonely drunk that adverbs should at least get a pass in dialogue. People *do* speak in adverbs, like constantly. Any number of people spew adverb upon adverb with no loss of face.

He suffered the mockery of Hemingway on every page. He attempted to pay deference with deletion, but he was weak and ended up quietly despising the Great One for ruining it for everyone else, and then that whole leaving things out to the point of leaving *everything* out. Owen's novels ran around seven-hundred pages, a mountain range of words. Whenever a book of his was remaindered (there's a word for you) he felt sad for the trees.

Midway down a page he noticed the word "kept" and it kept him from feeling too sorry for himself. Another confounded rule of English. Kept, slept, wept, leapt…okay, you lose an "e", you add a "t", or with "ea" you add a "t." We all have to live with that. Then where is "heapt" and "reapt"? He looked away from adverbs for a moment to castigate the arbitrary rules governing verbs.

Vivian came by and asked if he wanted another Manhattan.

"I certainly do," he said.

"Awesome," she said, which now made him think anew about adjectives. Do they ever really describe the thing they are meant to describe? Accurately?

23

Nine-Eleven

LORINE WENT TO Mexico as part of an art tour, with a group from Harper College, which is in Upstate New York, near Owego where she lived. They worked on small watercolors of quaint scenes in several villages. In her retirement she found art a rewarding way to pass the time.

The instructor was a manic middle-aged woman Lorine suspected was on drugs. She was, however, encouraging to the beginners and helpful with problems of perspective.

When the week was over, Lorine stayed on. She enjoyed the slow pace of Mexico and the warmth of the people she encountered there.

Some who had registered never even took the trip, sacrificing their deposits because they were too afraid or depressed to leave the country at that time, or to board a plane. Those who did participate, all but Lorine, were ready to go home at the end of it. They thought they should be spending their money in New York, not in Mexico. They'd been told by President Bush that spending money was the patriotic response to an attack by foreign terrorists. Go shopping, eat out. She had nothing against the President except for his annoying reminders that he was a leader. The more he said it, the less she believed him.

Lorine was old enough to remember President Roosevelt telling the people to save everything: tin foil, postage stamps, scrap metal. She doesn't recall mention of going shopping or to a restaurant. They grew Victory Gardens and shared the food.

She saw 9/11 as a terrible crime committed by small gang of bad men, a crime that could have been prevented had it been imagined. It was an act of war only if you wanted it to be. But she was only one old lady alone in Mexico painting watercolors.

At dusk, Lorine went to the plaza where the colors were soothing. There she watched the return of the starlings with their raucous calls.

24

Sleep Surfing

EVERY BAR IN Palm Springs is a gay bar, except for Melvyn's where it is always two o'clock in the morning, 1955. You don't go there to meet women but meet one Owen did on a hot afternoon in March. In truth, he had already met her by means of a misdialed text, which led to more texting, which evolved into…what? Rendezvous? Hook-up? Half-blind date? He had misgivings but the girl had driven in from Ventura. The least he could do is buy her a drink.

He arrived ahead of her and ordered a martini, Melvyn's signature cocktail. A few old actors were still creating moments. A retired criminal attorney defended the existence of golf courses sucking up water in the worst drought ever. A former showgirl explained how pastrami sandwiches happened only in New York City.

The girl from Ventura came in alone and sat two barstools away from Owen. He thought she must be Teresa because she was younger than anyone there. He and Dave the bartender were in a conversation about selfish people still watering grass and driveways.

She chimed in with, "The whole idea of a bourgeois lawn has outlived its charm, and anyway the desert is no place for a stupid lawn."

"You must be Teresa."

"You must be Owen."

"So you came."

"I guess I did. Did I make a mistake?"

"You tell me."

Dave didn't hear any of that and when he came back, he went on about summer still several weeks away, the annual test of endurance faced by people like them who remain in the desert year-round because they had no other place to go.

"Whenever you leave the house," Owen told Teresa, "you have to take a big hat, sunblock, and a liter of smartwater, and sip it all day. If you wait until you're thirsty it's too late. It's like Wyoming in reverse. Winter in Wyoming you stay inside. Summer in the desert, you stay inside. On the plus side, the snowbirds are gone and you can park anywhere."

"Thanks for the tip. Don't know how long I'll be here, though."

Owen was divorced by then and sad to face that now a woman in her thirties was too young for him. She never brought up the age difference when they started seeing each other, and soon she found a job and an apartment, and they were sleeping together. This proved to be a problem he did not expect. She was a snorer, world-class.

Snorers will always deny the affliction. For them it is not a problem. If it were only the snoring, he might be able to overcome it. She was nice to be in bed with but only until she fell asleep. In her sleep she kicked him, elbowed him, and often talked gibberish. One night she got out of bed, walked to the fridge, and ate a cold slice of pizza, all the while fast asleep. He held his breath watching her. It made him hesitant about becoming too attached to her.

He steered her to make love at her place but not his, because he wanted to be able to leave once she fell asleep. The sleep thing was something they would have to talk about eventually.

They were Happy Hour friends with benefits. Beyond that, he didn't know what they were and she didn't tell him.

He suggested they go out on a real date, dinner and a movie, and afterwards talk about what page they were on. Such a date was a step of sorts. He didn't know where, but he knew the general direction. An hour before they were supposed to meet at Spencer's, she called and said she was totally exhausted from work and all she wanted was to go to bed early.

The next morning, there she was on page one of The Desert Sun, crowd surfing at Tachevah, the city street party, her right fist up in the air, her left hand on somebody's head. She wore a halter, short shorts, and shower shoes, one hanging off her toes. Some dude with a backwards baseball cap had one hand on her ass, the other on the meaty part of her thigh, passing her across the outstretched hands of the crowd.

Owen was put out that she had blown him off, that she gave up dinner at a high-end place and a French film, "Les Gorilles," in favor of being tossed by strangers. She was too young for him. He would end it.

He called, waking her up. She seemed pleased that he called, but she usually was. It was her way.

"How was your night?" he asked.

"I slept around the clock! I was so exhausted!"

"And now?"

She failed to notice the accusing tone in his voice. She was bright and happy for another day.

"Still exhausted!" She laughed.

"When did you go to bed?"

"Seven! Seven PM to seven AM. I was, like, dead!"

He realized she was not lying. He held the phone to his chest, as though saying an aside to someone next to him, and in a way he was. He was telling himself it would be an adjustment, but life is full of adjustments.

"Let's have dinner tonight, then," he said, "and maybe a movie."

"Awesome!"

25

The Plunge

VINCE, 27, HAD a subsidized studio/loft across the river on Virginia Avenue, a good deal. He spent most of his time there, painting and listening to NPR, breathing in the fumes of oils and mediums and mineral spirits. He refused to switch to acrylics or water-based oils because they sucked in comparison to the rich buttery depth of true oils. An artist named Muriel, who was not bad, lived on the same floor, but she wasn't attracted to him, or to his art with its challenging colors. Few were.

Ongoing forums from San Francisco, KQED, discussed putting up some kind of barrier to prevent people from committing suicide by jumping off the Golden Gate Bridge, a magnet for the thus inclined. Like Vince. That particular bridge was not a locale in his fantasies, because he'd never looked down from it himself. For many others, however, it was the bridge of their dreams. Or nightmares. Reno had plenty of things to jump off, maybe not as pretty nor as high, but not without interest, and not unused. Like most American cities, Reno had a suicide hot line. Vince had called it twice. He said he was poor and thwarted and lonely and generally not good enough to garner happiness. Once he spoke to a woman, another time a man answered. They both told him that things would get better. So far, they hadn't.

With an MFA he could teach, but he doubted he'd be any good at it, and he was still under the weight of his college loan, something the government extended even to art majors. He often wondered if college was a good idea for him. He might have invested that money into a live-in studio, a web site, maybe even his own gallery.

He was, after all, already an artist when he went to college. What he got there was validation, and even that was dubious. Anytime the academy says you're good, you're probably not and you wind up sleeping on the sofa of a college friend and getting dental care in exchange for waiting room art, the painting of which hurt more than the tooth. He had no woman because he had no money. Though artists do at times become rich and famous while still alive, no woman was willing to bet that he would be one of them.

The first person to jump off the Golden Gate Bridge was a worker on the crew building it. If the city put up an effective barrier, someone would gain the distinction of being the last. The count so far is a secret, he heard, but the best guess is somewhere around two thousand. The last one would certainly be epic, unless he survived, but that is unlikely. A high school kid on a field trip took the leap on a dare, fully clothed and fully expecting to survive, which he did. Only a few others have and upon reflection, which began on the way down, decided it had been a mistake to jump.

Vince thought he could at least pack his sketchbook and have a look. He could take the bus.

26

Fame

IN LOS ANGELES the screenwriter stayed at The Sofitel, across from the Beverly Center. It smelled of French furniture polish, which made him think of Paris. At his studio meeting, the opening small talk was about his choosing to live in Reno instead of Los Angeles. They found that odd. The rest of the long day was spent listening to "The Creative Team" instruct him on the choices he made in his script, both good and bad. The producer, a functioning illiterate, wore everyone out with his manic energy. The studio people were intelligent but frightened for their futures, unlike the producer who was fearless. After the meeting, the screenwriter was reluctant to return to his hotel, which however nice its aroma was still lonely. He stopped at Barney's Beanery for a Jack Daniels and soda.

Two girls walked in together, one of them Japanese-American. That one sat next to him. She was pretty, and the white girl was all right, too. The girls chatted and giggled to each other and smoked, which was allowed then. The screenwriter never knew how to talk to girls in bars, so he sat quietly. He coughed, and the Japanese girl patted his back.

"You're the one smoking and I'm the one coughing," he said.

"I'm sorry, I'll put it out."

"No, I wasn't complaining. I meant the irony. I don't mind

smoke; I like the smell of it. Or maybe it's you."

"You like the smell of me?"

"I do. Would you like a drink?"

She turned away from her friend who was already engaged in conversation with the man who sat next to her.

He turned toward her, now knees almost touching, and he let her know that he was on the brink of fame, if he didn't implode.

"I'm used to meeting guys on the brink of fame. It's West Hollywood."

"So, everybody's like that?"

"Famous, used to be famous, or on the brink of it."

He ordered another round of drinks and leaned toward her and kissed her. No one noticed, not even the other girl.

The screenwriter fell into a monologue about "the moment" and how they might never meet again. She took it that he wanted some serious time with her.

"Give me a minute."

She turned back to her friend and used the minute to ditch her. They'd both done that before.

He drove her in his rented car to her apartment in Santa Monica. Once inside, she walked away from him, shedding her clothes. He had seen that scene before in movies and would never have written one like it.

In bed, she apologized for being a few pounds over her normal weight.

"You look good to me. You feel good. You smell good."

He did his best but couldn't bring her around. She gave him that pat on the back and said, "I'm a hard come." He'd heard that was a cultural thing with Japanese women, but of an earlier generation.

He saw her again two weeks later when he was in town to take another meeting, as the expression was and still is. This time they went out on a date, cocktails and dinner. They passed on dessert and went back to her place. It was much like the time before, which was good enough. He tried something else. It got her nowhere.

"But I liked it. I really did."

She called him a week later when he was back in Reno. The call was a pleasant surprise until the warning came that she might have passed an STD on to him. "The guy I slept with between those two times with you called me, so, you know, I'm calling you. You should call whoever."

"I don't have whoever to call," he said, "but thanks, I guess."

He never saw her again, and though his script became a hit movie, he never became famous. Just another guy at Barney's. This was when they still had that infamous sign: "No faggots allowed."

27

The Final Tally

JACKSON BECAME THE most famous of all American artists. His startling rise was fueled by the good graces of one influential art critic and one rich old woman, who convinced him that what he was doing was groundbreaking, masterful, and destined to enrich the culture. Not to mention enriching those in on the ground floor of speculating on his career.

It followed that he took a mistress, said by some to resemble Elizabeth Taylor. His wife, who resembled no one in particular, escaped his drinking and the mistress and her own humiliation and fled to Paris. On that same day the mistress moved in.

She shared with the artist the love of drinking and had aspirations of becoming an artist herself. One day she demanded of him, "Show me how you make a painting."

He gave her a demonstration and within half an hour produced an example of what he had discovered was the road to fame and riches. He presented it to her as a gift, the story goes.

After the artist killed himself and a young woman—not the mistress—in a car crash, his widow came back to America to settle his affairs, not the least of which was a painting in the possession of the former mistress, who desired to sell it for whatever the market would bear, which in the case of this artist was equal to the annual budget of Biloxi.

The widow and a panel of experts agreed that it looked in its finer points unlike the paintings the artist did when he did not know if he was painting or splattering. This one, to the expert eye, appeared to have been thought out.

Of all the experts who examined it, however, only the widow was willing to go on record and call it a fraud. Upset by that judgement and in dire need of money, the mistress insisted it was genuine, a love gift to commemorate Le Grand Affaire, an intense relationship of deep and abiding emotions.

"More like five fucks," said the widow, which suggests that though she had escaped to Europe, some line of communication with her husband had remained open.

28

Forever, For Now

FRANK CHECKED INTO L'hotel de la Place des Vosages, off rue St. Antoinne. He had to carry his large suitcase and a carry-on up to the first floor because the lift did not go down to the ground floor. The room was as small as the one he had had that first time in Paris, when he met and made love to the typewriter *méchanicienne*. He left his bags and walked to the apartment on the right bank where he would be living for the next month. The woman who owned the apartment, an American ex-pat friend of a friend, briefed him on the diet and habits of Rachel and Sophia, the two Siamese cats he would be caring for while she was on holiday in Barcelona. They all sat on the floor together for the introductions. The cats were satisfied with him. She gave him a key and he moved in the next morning, after she had gone.

The spacious apartment faced the Seine, which you could watch as you sat at the grand piano by the window. The living room gave the appearance of a small ballroom. At night Frank would turn up the radio and dance across the floor to Katy Perry's "I Kissed a Girl," wildly popular in Paris then.

He fell into a routine of rising at ten to feed Rachel and Sophia. After cleaning their litterbox, he would walk up to Blvd. Beaumarchais to the bakery Au Levain du Marais, where the croissants are delicious but small. He would buy two and eat one of them on the way to another cafe near the Bastille. At a table, he would eat the second croissant with a cafe creme.

On past trips he toured the monuments, museums and churches, as many as he cared to, so this time he devoted himself simply to walking the city he loved with no destination in mind.

At five o'clock he would return to the cats but first stop at Le Sully, which was close to the apartment. There he would have an afternoon pastis. The woman behind the bar would give him a tiny plate of olives with his Pernod. Fifty years before, with the French girl, he learned how to pronounce Pernod and how to drink it. During those five days they covered Deux Maggots, Lipp's, and Cafe Flores, as Americans do, so now he felt no need to go back to those places. He found his own cafes and spoke French in them, as well as he could, and thought he might stay in Paris forever, for now.

He felt conspicuous in restaurants, sitting by himself for two hours savoring three courses plus the cheese tray, so he decided to take his meals in brasseries where a person alone did not feel out of place.

In the evening the cats got their dinner and he danced alone to Katy Perry on the radio while they ate. He made emptying their litter box and brushing their fur a performance and urged them to participate. He enjoyed Rachel and Sophia. In their own aloof way they were good company, even though he preferred dogs. His wife had moved into his apartment to look after his while he was gone, a shaggy mongrel named Dumar.

29

A Nice Enough Life

BILL SAW EMMA, his ex-wife, for the first time in more than twenty years at the wedding of their son, Bill Junior. The usher led him to a seat next to her, on a bluff overlooking Puget Sound. They recognized each other but it took a moment. They exchanged polite greetings.

They sat in silence for a few moments, waiting for the event, until he asked her, "You think this is a good idea?"

"That's not for me to say. Where's Janine?"

"She thought it would be better if she didn't come."

"Oh, who cares at this point. She should have come. Bill will wonder where she is."

"She's back at the hotel."

"I don't know why she wouldn't come. Nobody's going to bite her."

"I'll tell her that. The wedding planners took a big risk on the weather, huh? Looks like they won. This'll photograph like a dream. Sometimes I miss the Northwest, living on the desert, but the heat is good for me."

"It is a beautiful day," Emma said. "Lucky."

"I wonder about it, though," he said.

"They're crazy in love. Hope for the best."

"I guess so." He knew he would have to propose a toast, say

a little speech, and he could wing that, but he had prepared something just for Emma. For himself, really. Now he hesitated, wondering what good it might do her, or what harm, but he went ahead and said what he'd planned to say. "My behavior back then was reprehensible. You deserved better. It's time I said I'm sorry."

She interrupted him to say, "I'm okay. No need to dredge it all up."

"I can rationalize it all, but I can't forgive it. I'm hoping you can, because it's put a stain on me."

She smiled. "Like spilling some soup on your shirt?"

"Worse than that."

"And my forgiving you would remove it, like bleach?"

"Probably not. Anyway, I'm truly sorry."

"Why now?"

"We might not see each other again."

"Okay, I forgive you."

"Really?"

"Sure, why not?"

He had hoped for something not so flip.

"You've been married a long time," she said. "Janine must have been good for you."

"Mostly. We've had our differences, but we've hung in." She nodded her approval. "And you're okay?"

"I've had a nice enough life," she said.

So, he nodded as well. The conversation stalled at this point, and Emma excused herself to stand up and walk to the back of the venue where her son and some others in the wedding party were fussing over something.

The forgiven took in a deep breath of salt air and listened to the harp.

30

The Middle of Something

AFTER COMPLETING HIS orientation as a new social worker, Darryl Jackson had only two weeks in the field before the Watts riots broke out. He was just getting a feel for the work, enough to learn that he was doing it all wrong. His job, it was explained to him, was to do no more than qualify or disqualify applicants for county aid. He was not obliged to comfort anyone nor ask personal questions like, "What were you in prison for?" and then joke that at least it qualified the applicant for the residency requirement. (It didn't, his supervisor smugly informed him.)

It took a few hours for the outrage in Watts to reach the point of no return. Shattered glass, looted stores, explosions, walls of fire, and shots fired. The National Guard descended on the area. By that time, Friday night, Darryl was already in Santa Barbara with a girl he'd been seeing. He was trying to fall in love with her. She made him feel comfortable in the world, and that was a good start.

They lay in bed watching the riot on TV. He had never lived in a city before and had never met a black person until college, but Los Angeles was his city now, and his clients and colleagues, mostly black, were trapped in the chaos of a riot, if not participating in it. By Sunday night, eleven o'clock news, Darryl could see he would not be returning to his shared room, which was within the curfew area, as was his office. He spent the next few days at the girl's apartment in Hollywood, where she made him an artichoke, his first, and taught him how to eat it.

The office reopened on Wednesday even though occasional bullets were in the air and fires were ablaze. Early that afternoon a bomb threat forced an evacuation of the building. Darryl and the other social workers milled about on the street waiting for the all-clear. Black, brown, white, and yellow, they agreed on one thing: the police did not know how to talk to or about black people. The Chief of Police described the protestors as "monkeys in the zoo."

Something unexpected happened out there on the street, a counterbalance to all that had happened before. A colleague named Helene put her hand on Darryl's arm and slipped a piece of paper into his hand. "What's this?" he asked.

"My address," she said. "If you find yourself trapped in the middle of something, try to get to my house. You'll be safe there."

He had had a secret crush on Helene from day one. She was beautiful, black as coal, with an assertive Afro, and more mature than he. They worked two desks apart from each other. He knew he didn't have a chance. This was in 1965.

That same night he walked alone from his car to her house on a deserted street in South Central, the smell of smoke still in the warm air. When she opened the door he said, "Seems like I'm always trapped in the middle of something."

Inside her house, he did not know what else to say, and she seemed unsettled so he kissed her. She must have liked it because she smiled.

"Are you crazy?" she said, "Walking around this neighborhood at night?"

"I didn't think about that. All I can think about is you."

She smiled at that, too. They kissed again and she led him into her bedroom.

When she came out of the bathroom, she walked toward the bed wearing only red panties, like a flame against her black skin. She lay down next to him and they embraced, his face pressed against hers. He apologized for the stubble on his face.

"I didn't know this would happen," he said. "I should have shaved."

She rubbed her cheek against his stubble and said, "It's the right feeling. And you knew."

"Dreamed, more like it."

He would have fallen in love with Helene, but she did not let him. It would be too hard to come back from, she told him. Come back where? he wondered.

On New Year's Eve, the last day of 1965, he married that girl he took to Santa Barbara. He moved out of the rooming house on Adams Boulevard and into her tidy apartment in Hollywood. It was a comfortable marriage but not a passionate one and it soon came to an end, to no one's regret.

31

Refuge

"I SEE IT as a good omen," June said, but that's the only kind of omen she ever saw. Owen envied that in her. He saw only the other kind. This was before they were married, when he was still struggling to find his own voice, hopeful of getting out of the influence of the great writers. They were in Havana, their first night in the forbidden city, there illegally by way of Cancun. Their spirits were high until they checked into the hotel and went up to their room. Owen had to go outside, walk it off.

"We could have at least unpacked our bags," she said.

"I need some time."

"Like, how much?"

"I don't know."

They had no map, so they walked nowhere in particular. On San Ignacio a tall Cuban man named Renaldo stood outside his entryway and invited them inside a crumbling paseo where he had set up a business selling hand-made percussion instruments to tourists. He urged them to try out the instruments, to play along with him, to make music together. June enjoyed the experience more than Owen did, but that was usually how it happened.

As residents of the apartments came in and out of the paseo Renaldo introduced them: This is my mother...my wife...my brother…my cousin. His house was their house, he told them, now and whenever. Owen wondered how sincere that sentiment was. If he told Renaldo about the hotel room, would he still invite him to take possession of his own place.

"We're at the Ambos Mundos," Owen told him.

"A fine hotel. Of course, I have never been inside."

"Room five-thirty-seven."

As though that should mean something to Renaldo, June thought, and why should it mean anything to Owen? It meant nothing to her. It would be a funny story when they went home. Why does he find every reason to torture himself? Back home he would tell everybody of his ironic fate. Room 537 of the Ambos Mundos, Havana, as though the room was contaminated. If Owen felt contaminated, that was his problem, not hers.

Renaldo turned the conversation back to the music of Cuba and said in a confidential whisper, "For us, you see, music is a refuge. Music and love. And sometimes rum."

June bought an instrument that made a rattling sound, something for her toddler niece. They said adios to Renaldo and walked in the general direction of their hotel.

"Honestly, I'm beat," she said. "Let's go back and unpack and go to bed. We can make Cuban love." But he was still in a mood. "I bet you anything he didn't write 'A Farewell to Arms' in that room. They just say that. People pay to go inside the room."

"No, he did. Right there. Next to us. They leave the door open so we can see where the magic happened, every time we go in, every time we come out."

"Maybe we can switch rooms. Or we can let it ruin our trip."

They did neither, credit to Cuban music, Cuban love, Cuban rum.

32

Everyone Swings with the Soft

FRANK WAS STILL wearing his Navy-issue peacoat with his honorable discharge in the pocket when he enlisted in a traveling circus. This transition was not meant to fulfill any boyhood dream. Not much about a mud show traveling through the American south is romantic. Maybe he needed to be part of a group again, one that would feed him and house him and not let him get too far lost. For the past four years he had been at sea and now he walked the earth uneasily.

He was a quick learner, though there was little to master in the art of shoveling elephant shit. He did, however, find the five unwritten rules of circus life profound:

1. Ten percent of a hundred dollars is seven dollars and fifty cents.
2. Never turn away a midget.
3. Chimpanzees are more dangerous than lions.
4. Everyone swings with the soft.
5. Everyone blows the show eventually.

Credit to that last one, the circus offers more opportunity for rapid advancement than any other business, show or otherwise. In the space of less than one season, Frank moved from shoveling elephant shit to the center ring where he became, "Captain Jeffrey Wainwright, fearless master of massive pachyderms!" That promotion came one day after the real trainer was sent to the hospital with injuries inflicted by a deliberate swipe of the trunk of one of his charges, in reaction to its being beat upon with a cattle prod.

The new job came with a considerable pay raise. The elephants knew what they were supposed to do, and they preferred Frank, who was kind to them and gave them onions by the bushel on a cold night. Although he became an overnight circus star, he still had to sleep in the bunk van, the black hole of circus working men. (Except in movies, they are never called roustabouts.)

Things went well and Frank wondered if he would lead by default the life of a circus performer. He calculated how long it would take him to save enough for his own camper van. He had not anticipated that the real trainer would return when his wounds healed. When that occurred Frank went back to shoveling shit.

During a two-day stand in Paducah the owner told Frank and Perry to take the pickup and go into town to buy new tires for the stake puller. Frank was put in charge.

The owner gave Frank a large greasy bag from the cook truck full of cash, ones and fives, to pay for the tires.

Having bought and loaded the tires, Frank gave ten percent of the money left over to Perry. (1.)

"Take the pickup and get these back to the lot," he told him.

"Where're you goin'?"

"I got something to do."

A midget who had watched their transaction heard they were from the circus. "Are they hiring?" he asked.

"They'll hire you. Go with Perry." (2.)

Frank watched them get into the truck. He called out a warning to the midget before they pulled away. "Stay away from the chimps!" (3.)

The midget looked confused.

Frank watched them drive away. He crossed the road and thumbed a ride in the opposite direction. (4., 5.)

33

Odyssey

JAMAL HAD A habit of hearing what was not said.

He met this Syracuse grad student one January night at the back entrance to The Straight when she backed into someone's car and pretended that it didn't happen. He called her Crash Collins and made her laugh. They had a couple beers and talked about nothing of any significance. He never asked what she was doing at Cornell, because he didn't care. He wasn't all that attracted to her. When he said goodnight in the parking lot, she opened the passenger door and with the gesture made her intentions clear. He woke up next to her in Syracuse.

It's not that he felt bad about it, it's that something felt wrong, like drinking eggnog in July.

She made him coffee and toast while he made a sign: "Ithaca." She drove him to a good place for hitching a ride.

His cheerlessness made her feel like she failed at something. When he wouldn't smile on demand she said, "Okay, I smile for you."

Then she left him by the side of the road.

What Jamal heard, though, was, "Ice mile for you."

It foretold, he was sure, a long cold way to go.

34

The View from Here

HARRY IS ON the cusp of becoming certifiably old.

In the mirror he does at times seem a stranger to himself.

Louise hasn't changed, at least not this view along her naked back.

Among vistas gone from memory are similar terrains on women not his wife.

He forgets what he was about to say, and the reason for entering that room, opening that drawer.

He seldom knows the date and forgets important ones.

He mixes up the names of his grandchildren.

He has to ask who Sandra Bullock is.

He dreads that one day he may forget how to breathe.

But at the moment he is breathing hard, and his heart is racing, with possible consequences he does not fear and would, in fact, welcome.

Yes! Yes! Yes! Oh, God, he will never forget this.

And so what if he does?

He is alive and at the apex of living. This moment here, now, no matter what will be remembered or what may be forgotten.

35

The C Word

CHRISSY, AMY'S MOTHER, looked resplendent in a navy-blue dress. She had taken care to present herself as an attractive woman aging well, while trying not to compete with her own daughter. It was, after all, her day. But where *was* she?

The harpist was getting on Chrissy's nerves.

She took a sidelong glance at her husband's head and found it translucent, as though he had had some work done, which he hadn't. She had. He was a good and decent man. He provided, he was undemanding, but he was no more than a man, given to the bad habits of men, revolving around matters of sleep, smoke, and sex. She wondered how she came to need him and when she no longer did.

The venue was outside, overlooking Puget Sound.

Bill Junior, the young man about to marry her daughter, if someone could discover her whereabouts, leaned toward his own mother and conferred. He was handsome but how far could that and a degree in communications take him? And Amy with her degree in art history. They would *starve* and blame each other.

She looked at Bill's father, whom they had never met, sitting alone and staring into space.

"I wonder if Bill Junior will turn out like his father," she whispered to Bob.

"Most people wind up like their fathers. It's an unwanted legacy."

A voice beside them: "Beautiful day for a wedding, ain't it?"

Uncle Vern, Chrissy's ne'er-do-well brother, was kneeling like a penitent in the aisle next to them. He had not been invited and wasn't expected to show up. They doubted he even had a driver's license. He lived off the grid with the perverse pride such people have about that.

"What the hell are you doing here?" Chrissy hissed.

"Couldn't stay away."

"You might as well take a seat," said Bob, who tried to keep the peace whenever Uncle Vern showed up.

"No, thank you, just came to tell you Amy's decided on something else. She's going in a different direction."

The parents went numb. The harp sounded vaguely Asian. The air smelled too salty.

"Where is she?" asked Chrissy with a steely urgency.

"Not here, sister."

"We can see that. Everybody can see that. It's excruciating."

Uncle Vern laughed at the word. "Cancer of the asshole is excruciating."

"Did you have a hand in this?" demanded Bob, giving up his role as peacekeeper. "Because if you did, I swear I'll kill you."

"Me? I'm not even considered a member of the family. Crazy old Uncle Vern. Only one ever took me seriously was that girl."

"God, and why?" said Chrissy.

"We were pals. We spoke the same lingo."

"Just tell us where she is and go away."

"Don't know for sure but I'm guessing on a plane to Caracas."

"Caracas!"

"Left all the coffee gadgets behind in their gift boxes."

"She called you for advice?" said Bob.

"She did. Not the first time either, surprise! All I told her was she was free to do anything, anything at all. She could marry up at such a tender age, or she could get on a plane and go somewhere. Something you could have done, too, sister, by the way."

A devout atheist, Uncle Vern made the sign of the cross, groaned as he stood upright, and said, "You're welcome."

In their despair over the ruination of an event months in the planning and expenses approaching six figures, Chrissy and Bob turned toward each other and uttered the same word: "Caracas," loud enough so that people nearby fell silent and looked at them.

"It's a metaphor," Uncle Vern explained before retreating up the aisle.

36

Italy

THE NEXT MORNING, Vince ran into Georgio at the front desk of his depressing hotel in Milan. Georgio could see that Vince was sad and urged him to join him later for lunch.

Georgio showed up at the Piazza Duomo with a tall South African writer he had moments before befriended. The three of them had lunch together. The writer, who was looking forward to becoming an American after his travels, told them a joke current in his home country: "What do you call a patriot in South Africa? Someone unable to sell his home."

The day before, coincidentally, Georgio—and this may have been what brought them together—had taken the long flight from Johannesburg to Milan via Zurich. "You will notice," he said, "that I am wearing the same suit and shirt that I wore yesterday. I have been in these clothes for three days." He explained that he had taken his girlfriend from Rome to Johannesburg to break up with her. (Her parents lived there.) He then hurried back to the airport, leaving his luggage behind.

He met Vince, he told the writer, the night before, when he had to intervene on his behalf in a curbside dispute with a taxi driver.

"The driver picked me up at the railroad station..." Vince began.

"Stazione Centrale."

"…and drove me around the block to the hotel. He wanted twenty-five euros for the ride."

"An outrage. The driver was probably from the south."

"I'd taken the train from Paris." Vince's distaste for Italy began at that moment, but out of courtesy he kept that to himself. "We settled at fifteen, thanks to Georgio."

"Too much, still," said Georgio. "Highway robbery. The driver was from the south, I'm sure. You cannot trust anyone from the south."

It was Sunday and the stores were closed, which depressed Vince as much as the taxi and the hotel. He had thought arriving by train on a Saturday night would lift his spirits but no such luck. They lingered over lunch for five hours, a distraction which might have saved Vince from suicide. The writer went on about his second book, the research for which would take *years*. His first book was a warm-up. His goal was to outdo James Michner, his idol. The book would cover Italy over generations, perhaps centuries. The title would be "Italy" and he estimated it would weigh in at three and a half pounds.

Georgio admitted he was a businessman, second in line to the family business.

"And what do you do?" the writer asked Vince.

"I'm a color-blind artist from Reno, Nevada."

They were curious, of course, but Vince deflected any tests of vision by asking about Georgio's family business.

His family, Georgio told them, had a factory in Genoa that made parts for the oil industry. What kind of parts he did not elaborate on. He invited them to come spend a day on the family's boat.

The writer was excited about the invitation and wanted right then to set a day when they could all meet in Genoa. Vince, though, was not sure. There was something about Georgio that was at the same time outgoing and secretive. During the long lunch he excused himself several times to go to the toilet, disappearing for fifteen minutes at a time. Once when the interval seemed unreasonably long, Vince went after him, worried he said that Georgio might be sick. Vince returned to the table and told the writer, "We might have lost Georgio."

They thought about paying the bill and leaving but Georgio's sunglasses were still on the table. They waited over another coffee and Georgio eventually returned.

Vince asked him outright where he had gone. He smiled and said, "Can you guess?"

"No, I have no idea."

The writer suggested that some girl must have caught his eye.

"Exactly!"

Vince did not believe that. It sounded like a hustler's gambit. If you want to evade a question, ask for a guess, and then make that your answer, already plausible by the guess.

The evening promenade began, young girls stylishly dressed and boys wearing T-shirts with incongruous English words on them. "Stanford Fire Truck Line," for example.

Georgio insisted on paying the bill. "I pay," he said, as though he always paid. Vincent and the writer resisted but not forcefully. "I know a place very nearby that serves a special grappa, an unbelievable grappa. Please, be my guests in a delightful experience. You will not be disappointed."

Again, the writer was eager to accept, but Vince had had grappa before. It tasted like jet fuel. Besides, the element of distrust had taken root in him. Still, he went with them. Vince, after all, had started his European trip with a notion, if not a plan, that he would not return.

They joined the promenade for half a loop.

In the center of the floor of the galleria is a mosaic of a legendary bull.

Once informed of the tradition, Vince stepped on the bull's

balls for good luck. He followed behind two men he did not know into the dusk of a strange city in a foreign county.

37

Seattle, Miami

FRANK WAS WELL aware that what he was doing was wrong, but he didn't know what else he could do. His wife, from whom he was separated, had plans to take his son to *Turkey*. A six-year-old boy to Turkey? Ten days in Turkey? What kind of vacation is that, with all that was happening over there? Turkey is a dangerous place. Not that Oakland isn't, but a single woman with a small boy would do better to stay in Oakland. And who knows if that is where she really intends to go, or how long she might stay. She didn't always tell the truth.

She would say it was kidnapping. The law would agree. If he had to go to prison over this, he would never see Guy. If he did nothing, he would have to hold his breath and hope for their safe return and settle for the usual every other weekend, a tradition that puts a father's heart into a cage. At least it *was* every other weekend, and the month of July. They could practice kicking the football. They could pretend. They could dream. Or they could continue driving north on Route 5 into an uncertain future.

She allowed him to pick up their son after pre-school, and she expected they would stop for fro-yo or a burger. It's possible she won't call the police right away. Even if he turned around right *now*, he would still have a three-hour drive, and he already told Guy they were going to Seattle.

"When will we get to Seattle?" the kid asked.

"It's a long way off. We'll have to stay in a motel tonight. I'll find us a fun place with a pool."

If they were stopped by the police for any reason, he could picture Guy telling the cop that they were on their way to Seattle. That might lead to some questions he was not prepared to answer. Neither he nor his son, however, realized that what each of them was saying was not what the other one was hearing.

They stopped at a rest stop, and he helped his little boy stand at the urinal. On the way back to the car, Guy asked again, "When will we get to Seattle, Dad?"

"I don't really know, kid. Sometime tomorrow. What's the rush?"

"Who is Attle anyway?"

Frank could not help laughing. They sat for a while on a bench. The rest stop had a pay phone.

"Let's call your mom."

"Okay."

He called Kiran. Her voice was chilly, demanding to know where they were. He apologized and said, "We've been driving around and lost track of time, looking for Mister Attle."

"Who?"

Frank took the next exit and headed back south.

When he finally did drop off his son, Kiran was both relieved and angry. Guy was asleep in Frank's arms.

As it turned out, Kiran cancelled the trip to Turkey and took their son to Florida instead.

Guy excitedly told his father, "We're gonna go see my Ami!"

38

The Gift

THAT MANY SO gay men are named Bruce cannot be denied
or explained. This particular Bruce, an earnest young man, had
a partner of five years, who the week before had asked for his
hand in marriage. Speechless, Bruce could do no more than look
at the offered ring as though it were an oddity of nature. His
impulse was to say yes, but he had already spent some time
thinking around the subject without sharing his thoughts. He
wondered how many of their friends were getting married solely
because now they could, buying into a tradition long prohibited
to them, not to mention often ridiculed by them. Accept a
tradition and you buy into all of it, thought Bruce, or what's the
point? Forsaking all others, until death do us part, the sickness
thing, the sharing thing. (That part was appealing because his
partner was a podiatrist with a successful practice and Bruce was
a retail clerk at Stein Mart making a bit over minimum wage.)

Bruce reasoned that just because you knocked down the
gate did not mean you had to go jump into the lake.

The podiatrist, on bended knee, was hurt that the silence
lasted so long, revealing an uncertainty he did not expect. To
ease the pain on both sides he back-pedaled and said, "Take some
time, honey, think it over. We have a strong commitment, I know,
and if you don't want to take the next step…"

He stopped short of an ultimatum.

Refolding some towels in the home department and lost in his own misgivings, Bruce heard a gentle voice say, "Excuse me?"

"Yes, ma'am, can I help you?'

"I hope so," said the elderly lady. "I need a hostess gift, but I don't know what would be appropriate."

Bruce welcomed the distraction and enjoyed whenever his opinion was sought on matters of style and motif.

"Well, tell me a little something about the hostess," he said.

"I don't know that much about her, honestly. She's younger than I by about ten years. I haven't had sight of her in...decades, but back then she was quite attractive."

"Hmmm, that's not much to go on."

"She's my ex-husband's wife. I don't know her that well. I hardly know her at all."

"And she's hosting you...?"

"Just for the night. At their house. I would have preferred to stay at a hotel, but I'm on a fixed income and it wasn't cheap getting down here from Seattle."

"May I ask the occasion?"

"Bill, my ex, is dying. He asked to see me."

Bruce needed a moment to absorb that.

"And you said yes?" he finally asked. "I mean, I guess you said yes, you're here."

The lady nodded. "I'm sure Janine would rather I not come. She's in an awkward position, don't you think?"

"I would say so. But so are you."

"I'd like to get her something to, you know, ease the awkwardness."

"How long ago was the split?" Bruce asked, though that had nothing to do with the choice to be made in the home department.

She had to think for a moment. "Thirty-some years?" Longer than Bruce has been alive. "He left me for her. Seems to have worked out."

"How long were you married?"

"Twelve years."

"Did you remarry?"

"Oh, no. I didn't want to go through that again."

"But he left you…"

"That's why I didn't want to risk it again."

"…and after all these years, he wants to see you again…and that's okay with you?"

"When you love a man enough to marry him, you pretty much love him for life, ready or not."

"Really?"

"I thought about getting flowers, but she might have allergies. Lord, it seems everybody does these days. I'm lucky in that department. So, what have you got here that might work?"

Bruce advised her that candles were so yesterday and linens were a tad too intimate, wine glasses too suggestive, and cutlery just plain wrong. In the end he recommended a set of bamboo placemats. She thought that sounded perfect. She thanked him and took her placemats to the front of the store, to the cashiers. He hurried into the men's room and called his boyfriend, catching him between patients.

"Yes. Let's do this thing."

39

Ascension

ON THEIR SIXTH date, twice as long as it should have taken by current standards, Alvin got to sleep with Sara. She took the initiative. It was like finding something he didn't realize he'd lost, something he wasn't sure existed in the first place.

In the afterglow, he thought, this must be love. This is what was missing, all that was missing. He wanted it to go to where love could take you, but how could he ever fit into her world?

Sara ran marathons. She climbed mountains. She travelled alone to distant lands with no more than a backpack. She *camped out*. For Alvin, leaving the house for any reason required a long interior dialogue full of cruel recriminations and shaky assertions, and then once outside he didn't know where to go or what to do if he got there.

Could they live a romantic life together sharing hopes and fears and dreams and more fears?

One day he told her, as though presenting credentials: "I can make toast."

She replied: "I can bake bread."

Their love affair ended shortly after that, as Alvin knew it would. How could it not? He had nothing to offer a woman like Sara. The memory of the brief affair clung to him going forward, one more layer of regret.

When he heard that she fell off the face of El Capitan while attempting to scale it, the loss found a place in the pattern of his larger grief.

In his later years he thought of her every time he struggled up a flight of stairs.

40

Rock Star

HOMES IN LOS Angeles, at least the ones the Reno screenwriter had been invited into, mirrored the outside—light and airy. In Paris it was the same way, if the rock star's apartment on the Ile Cité were any example. It was as cold and dark inside as Paris was outside, that first week in December. A portable heater sat in the middle of the living room, laboring to take away the chill, with only minimal effect.

They met for the first time the previous night over dinner at a Chinese restaurant. In Paris, but it was a favorite of the rock star. Afterwards, they walked some boulevard, the idol's long overcoat billowing behind him. Although he was recognized by everyone they passed, no one tried to stop the music icon for a picture, an autograph, a word. The French. They went to the screenwriter's hotel room and over the course of the evening emptied the minibar, then smoked what weed was left in the pockets of that billowing overcoat. Outsized original ideas cascaded upon them. "Take notes!" cried the star, in his British accent. "This is gold!" The screenwriter tapped his temple. No notes, especially on anyone's demand.

His Ile Cité living room was cavernous and sparsely furnished with dreadful antique French furniture. He and his supermodel wife were camping there while a chateau was being built for them somewhere outside of the city.

The ideas that were so golden the night before were like lead in the morning. All the screenwriter had were the same bare bones he had started with, conceived by the singer himself: a rock star's life of debauchery is upended by the appearance of an unknown twelve-year-old son in the uniform of a military academy. It was the kind of storyline that reminds you of things you were sure you've seen before.

The week in Paris was arranged by Warner Brothers for the screenwriter to hang out with the rock star to see if he could do something new with the idea. Maybe the studio wanted to create some chemistry between them that might give life to something better. The important thing was to get that rock star on a movie screen.

What to say? Who was the mother? Did she die? Was she seeking revenge by foisting this strait-laced pre-teen upon a rock 'n roll star who is among the worst role models imaginable? The characters remained fleshless, so they turned to casting. The star would play the lead, of course, but he did not want to give the impression it was about him.

"Everybody will think it is about you," said the screenwriter.

"You'll have to find a twelve-year old," said the rock star. "I've seen child actors that blow my mind."

"The woman's role feels small," said the screenwriter. "Maybe non-existent."

So, who else is in it? The obligatory entourage. Fast women, sleazy promoters, drug dealers. What happens after the first act? The father teaches the son how to have a good time? The son gives the father the moral compass he never had? Their conversation flagged. They were boring each other.

The singer picked up The Wall Street Journal, which had been lying on that uninviting sofa. The screenwriter did not want to watch someone read the paper. He asked about the album the band was putting together in Paris.

The star came to life then and played a track, one that went on for a long time with a repetitive refrain. He put aside The Wall Street Journal, got to his feet, and danced to the music with moves so much his own they bore his name.

This moment, an unknown writer watching a rock legend dance to his own music in a dank Paris living room, is the movie, thought the screenwriter. The other one would come to nothing.

41

Local Politics

THE DAY AFTER the city council meeting Stewart had coffee with his friend, Bob, who didn't get involved with issues. The friend asked him a one-word question: "Well?"

"We will continue to have our bones rattled by leaf blowers and other assorted garden polluters. Why? Because, '…those are hard-working guys.' I'm a hard-working guy, too, but they don't give a shit about my work."

"Nobody does. You're a poet."

"You don't think that's work?"

"You don't have to show up anywhere."

"Exactly. I have to work at home, and I can't because everybody wants leaves to stay in the trees. What's unnatural about leaves on the ground?"

"You came closer than anyone else. Everybody else gave up. Look at it like that."

"I'm not going to look at it at all."

"You can't beat city hall."

"Did you just say that?"

"Everybody says that."

"My mistake was in ever giving up my cynicism."

"You gave it up?"

"I'll get it back."

"I'm not sure you ever had it."

"I thought I did."

"You don't want to be a cynic. It's unlikeable. A poet ought to be likeable. It's good to be a skeptic, though."

"I can see the distinction. Thank you. I'm skeptical about that city council and that mayor."

"Did you get up and speak?"

"Of course, I got up and spoke. Then I sat there and gave the mayor the old stink-eye. His scrawny throat went dry, had to pour himself a drink of water."

"You should of gave him a beer and a hot dog."

They laughed at the shallows of their mayor's corruption.

"You got closure at least," said Bob.

"Now you say closure? Out loud?"

"It's a thing."

"Who came up with 'closure'?"

"Not me."

"Then don't say it."

"You gonna let this eat away at you?"

"Looks like."

"I thought born-again Buddhists didn't hold grudges."

"Only for one lifetime. It'll pass quickly."

42

Harry and Louise Make a Sex Tape

BY THE TIME Harry got Louise to agree to make a sex tape, technology had advanced beyond tape. And Harry's comprehension. Harry, 82, had argued for a sex tape back in the days of VCR, when Louise's body and sexual skills seemed to cry out for documentation, but even after seven years of marriage, she did not trust her husband with naked pictures of herself.

"It would be something just for the two of us," Harry tried to persuade her, but no woman with any imagination was going to buy that.

"No means no," she said.

And so the notion evaporated.

That which evaporates, however, also condenses. Harry made the discovery that his new iPhone could take videos as well as still pictures which can be deleted at will.

He reignited the request, and since his phone was locked with a password that only she could remember and his thumb print was unreliable, Louise, 78, thought, what the hell? How much could you see on that tiny screen anyway?

As director, Harry made the choice to shoot the documentary poolside where the light would be better, and the theme might be Summer Frolics. He was delighted to discover in the process that his phone video also had sound.

More time was required to set up the camera than to shoot the scene, a truism of film making. Harry had to brace his iPhone against the box it came in atop a box of Bran flakes, fixing it on a tilt with a strip of scotch tape. As he worked on these necessary steps, he said, "Remember, we have sound, so you should make some noise, a little moaning and dirty talk."

Louise rolled her eyes.

It played out in five scenes with a running time of seventy-two seconds. Scene One: Louise fluffs what looks like an awakening erection and Harry guides her to her elbows and knees. Scene Two: Our protagonist approaches success. "Oh, yes, baby! You like that? You want more of that?" Scene Three: The reversal. "You're not in." Scene Four: The catastrophe. Louise's knee slides and hits the hard edge of the chaise. "That's my new one!" she cries. Scene Five: The resolution. She rolls over and she's moaning all right, but not in the way Harry had hoped to hear it. She takes his flaccid member in her hand for a take-two. Nothing. She looks up at him with patient forbearance. And, scene.

They watched the rough cut together, feet dangling in the pool. Each had notes.

"The wind jiggled the camera," said the director.

"Skinny legs and sagging asses," said the star. She tossed the iPhone into the water.

Harry, with no further comment, watched it sink to the bottom like a penny thrown into a wishing well.

43

Splitting Eights

THE SCREENWRITER SAT third to the deal, the brim of his Bailey hat lowered to block out any view of the dealer, who had been running a stand-up routine based on the accident of his birth, like so many other comedians.

His particular source of humor was that he was from South Jersey. People from South Jersey sometimes confuse being loud with being funny. The routine would never be allowed in Vegas, where dealers are trained to shut up and deal. Still, the player wouldn't trade half of Reno for two of Vegas. An annoying human dealer is still better than an inoffensive robot. He enjoyed talking to most of the Reno dealers, like Lorena with the blessed breasts or the funny Asian woman who married a Texan and came to regret it.

The vacant seat next to him was taken by an overweight bearded man wearing a Rolex, his fist tight around a handful of chips. He laid down a five-dollar chip. When Jersey busted, the new player was overly elated. He was fifty-something. He also wore Jimmy Choo glasses.

On the next deal Rolex flashed his fourteen and asked the screenwriter should he risk a hit.

"Yeah," was the answer.

"But the dealer's showing a king."

"I see that."

The hit was a seven and now the screenwriter was his new best friend.

"I don't play cards much since what I do for a living is enough of a gamble. This is my first time in Reno. How about you?"

"I live here."

"Really?"

"People do."

"I live in LA. I'm a producer."

"TV or movies?"

"Both. I had meetings in 'Frisco and thought, what the hell, rented a car and drove here. Cleared my head."

No one asked him what he had produced. 'Frisco? Who says that?

"Who are your three favorite screenwriters?" asked the player during the shuffle.

The question threw the producer.

Was a civilian testing his credentials?

It was a question he never thought about because no one had ever asked before. Unless you're part of the industry most people can't even name three screenwriters. Rolex gave it some thought. The dealer offered him the cut. He cut the deck and named his three favorites: Charlie Kaufman, Alvin Sargent, and the man who had asked the question.

"What's so special about him?"

The producer was surprised to be having this conversation in Reno of all places. Cards flew across the felt and landed in front of the players.

The screenwriter looked at his hole card.

"He writes from the heart," said the producer.

"So do the other two."

"Which makes them special in this town. That town, I mean."

"Whatever happened to him?" asked the screenwriter, a question he often asked himself.

"Crashed and burned. Disappeared." He flashed his hand again, two eights, and asked, "Should I split them?"

"By all means. How does a writer disappear…"

"In Hollywood? You wake up one morning."

"…when he's already invisible?"

"The dealer has a face card showing."

"I see that."

"Should I split them anyway?"

"Always and forever, you split eights. Put up another chip."

He increased his bet and on the first card he drew a two.

"Now what?"

"Now you got ten, so you can double down on that hand, too."

Rolex slid forward another chip and was dealt a card face down. He turned the end of it up and looked at it, embarrassing everyone at the table.

The dealer flipped a card on the other eight. Another two.

"Now you have to go double-down on that one, too."

Excited, the producer put down another five. Now he had twenty dollars on the game and was on the edge of his seat. Again, he looked at the hole card. One of the other players could not suppress a groan. Nobody ever looks at the hole card in a split.

"I've got twenty in both of them!" the producer crowed. "Thanks for your help, bro."

The dealer turned over his hole card. A six. He drew a five. Twenty-one. The producer watched his chips scraped away.

"That wasn't such a good idea."

"It's not an idea. It's what you do with eights. So how come you never made a movie with any of those three screenwriters?"

"How do you know I didn't?"

The dealer reshuffled.

"Did you?"
"No, they're all heart and no money."
With that he cut his losses and left the table.

44

Short Flight

OWEN OPENED HIS book after the other two passengers in his row were settled. He read it during the boarding process, the taxi, and the take-off, a part of the trip that always seems longer than it has to be.

The woman in the middle seat leaned toward him as the plane was still climbing and said with a nervous smile, "Is that a good book?"

"Yes, it is," Owen said. It was an old Modern Library edition he found in a used bookstore.

She was Hispanic, in her early or middle twenties, and not with the man sitting in the window seat. "What's it about?" she asked, still smiling nervously. It was a short flight and Owen did not expect to chat about a book he was reading. "It's a collection of Russian short stories. I'm working on some short stories myself."

"You're a writer?"

"Yes."

"I'm sorry to bother you."

"That's all right. The short story is a difficult form and the Russians are good at it."

"How long is a short story?"

Great question. He was sure she did not care, and he could

only dream that she was coming on to him. Younger women seemed to like him for some reason, but he was old enough to be her father.

"No one knows. Too long and the reader might think it's not worth the investment. Too short and…well, I'm not sure if it can be too short. Hemingway insisted that a story becomes better with each thing you can cut out of it. He wanted to write a story where he cut *everything* out, but he never said what you would be left with."

"Is he your favorite?"

"No, I hate him. He contaminated a whole generation of writers, my generation."

"Please…I don't want to be a bother, but would you mind? Can you talk me through this?"

"Through what?" he asked.

"I hardly ever fly. This is the first time since my baby was born. To be honest, I'm terrified."

Owen shut his book. The plane was still soaring upward.

"No reason to be," he said. "Air travel is a pain in the ass but it's still the safest way to go."

"I know, I've heard that. But it doesn't lessen the fear."

"Bicycling is dangerous, flying is a breeze." He got a shaky laugh out of her. "I was eighteen before I ever flew and on my very first flight the plane caught on fire. Guys were on the tarmac in white body suits with hoses."

"Maybe you're not the best one to do this."

The man sitting at the window was wired up. It would have to be Owen.

"But that was a military plane. Next day we got back on that same plane and had as nice a flight as you can have on an Air Force plane."

"Thank you for your service."

"You're welcome. Listen, by the time we level off it'll already be time to prepare for landing. This is a short flight." She looked as though she didn't believe him. "I know, can't be short enough. Like a Hemingway story. What puts you on this flight?"

"I live in San Francisco. I work for a non-profit. They're sending me to Palm Springs for a conference. I didn't want to go, but how could I say no. It was meant to be a reward."

"I was in the East Bay for a few days, visiting my son. We went to see a Giants game. It was so cold we had to wear parkas. I prefer the desert heat."

The plane leveled off, the roar of the engines softened, and she relaxed a bit. Owen didn't know what to say to a scared girl with a baby at home. He offered to buy her a drink, but the flight was too short for beverage service. He asked her about her baby. Six months old, a girl. Her in-laws were taking care of her. Her husband worked. By then the descent had begun.

"Now, one thing I have to tell you," he said, "every time I've ever landed in Palm Springs it got a little rough, because of desert winds. But you just roll with it."

"Roll with it?"

"I mean, don't stiffen up, stay loose. This is a good plane with an experienced crew."

"How do you know?"

"I make this trip a lot. I know them personally. Now, the winds make the plane shake, things'll rattle, but then before you know it, you're safe on the ground. I'll be right here with you. I'm not going anywhere. Well, I'm going to Palm Springs, but we will get there together, safe and sound."

The winds hit them as he said they would and everything on the plane rattled. She gripped the armrests.

"It sounds worse than it is."

He patted her hand. She grabbed his and squeezed it. He was surprised by the pressure of her grip.

"Does your baby smile and laugh a lot?"

She nodded in jerking motions.

"I love that. Show me her picture. I'm sure you have a

bunch."

She was too scared to show him anything.

"You wonder what goes on in their little heads," he said. "Peek-a-boo, hands on the face, is sure-fire. Cracks them up every time."

He took his hand away and demonstrated. "Peek-a-boo!" She laughed, nearly hyperventilating. "I see you!" He played the game several times, then told her to notice that the shaking had stopped. The plane landed lightly on the tarmac and soon they were at the gate.

As they waited to disembark she showed him pictures of her baby girl.

"She looks just like you," he said.

"Thank you."

"There's never any wind on the way back north, so you'll be fine."

"Thank you."

45

Placemats

JANINE HAD HIM in the guest room, a plastic bucket within reach. Pill containers were lined up on the bedside table. Emma would not have put him in the guest room. She would have kept him in the master bedroom and stayed there with him, but he was not her husband anymore. Janine could do whatever she wanted.

She entered the sick room behind Janine, who trilled, "Sweetie, look who's here!" Janine busied herself by tidying up the room, but "Sweetie" asked her for some iced tea for their guest. She left reluctantly.

"Janine looks good. Hasn't changed a bit."

"She takes care of herself."

Talking did not come easy to him now. It never did, but that was a characteristic. Now it was physically exhausting.

"I'm so sorry you have to go through all this," she said.

"Wouldn't be my choice, but…"

"No, nobody wants…"

"Thanks for coming all this way."

"Sure. Are you in much pain?"

"It's not so bad."

She didn't know what else to say. What mutual friends they once had were dead or out of touch, and her life was of no interest to him now. The last time they talked was at their son's disastrous wedding, when he struggled to offer her an apology and she forgave him for the whole business. She did not expect to see him again until the next big event in somebody else's life. She understood that he needed her to sit with him one last time. Simple as that.

A TV set was on the bureau.

"You watching your sports in here?" she asked.

"Sometimes. Looks like the Dodgers might have their year. Only the Dodgers always look that way. They'll come in second again."

"The Mariners are another story altogether," she said. They both smiled, remembering baseball when they were together and lived not far from the King Dome.

She sipped her tea. The air conditioning made her uncomfortable. She looked forward to stepping back into the heat.

He said, "This is late coming, but I owe you an apology."

"Bill, you already did that, remember? At Bill's wedding? What was supposed to be his wedding."

"You didn't deserve all that."

"You said that, too, and I said it was so long ago. You said you were sorry, and I said okay."

"We won't be seeing each again."

"Everything sorts itself out in the end."

"Don't it?"

"Please don't dwell on those days, okay?"

"Okay."

She was relieved.

"You're lucky to have Janine to look after you."

"I know."

"I brought her a gift," she said. "She hasn't opened it yet. I'm thinking now it might not be the right thing."

"What is it?"

"Bamboo placemats. Ten of them."
"She'll use 'em. She'll use all of 'em."

46

The Touristas

IT WAS UNSETTLING to watch another man undo the buttons of her blouse. Jamal hadn't done it that often himself. They were still new to each other. If only the other man were her lover and he the voyeur. He regretted having asked her to go with him to Mexico.

She gave all the appearance of a dying woman. Her eyes fluttered like something was leaving her body.

Dr. Francisco, called by the hotel, listened to her heart and asked in an accent, "Is she taking any medication?"

"I don't know."

"Does she have any conditions or allergies?"

Jamal tightened his lips and repeated, "I don't know."

The doctor was an older man, past the age when most doctors in the states pack it in. He looked at Jamal in a disapproving way.

"To be honest," Jamal said, "I don't know her that well. It's the *touristas*, though, right? Everybody gets them."

"Do you have them?"

"No, but..."

As the doctor continued his examination, Jamal surfed his iPhone looking for information on what to do when you're with a new girl in Mexico, way down in Oaxaca, and she gets seriously sick. What popped up was how to deal with a death in another country, the formalities and the decision either to transport the body back home or to bury it in-country. He didn't know who her parents were or where they lived or who gets to decide what, under the circumstances. All he knew about her—and what attracted him most to her—was that she was up for anything. Like this spur of the moment trip to El Dia del Muertos.

"Doc? It's nothing serious, right?"

"Her blood pressure is very low. And, see, her color. She is turning yellow."

He looked up from his phone and peered at her skin, which two days ago felt so good against his own. He started a search for "yellow + skin." Jaundice, from the Greek word via the French word…bilirubin…hepatitis…whites of the eyes. He tried to look at her eyes, but they were closed. The last time he looked into them she seemed to be blaming him for everything.

"Look here," said the old doctor. He lifted her foot. The sole was yellow-orange.

"Oh, sweet Jesus!"

"How long has it been this way?"

"I have no idea. I never looked at her feet."

"No, I understand. Why would you?"

"Do something! Can't you do something? Should she go to the hospital?"

"Best not to move her."

Not to move her? He had a full schedule for Monday. He had to get back to San Francisco, but he couldn't leave her alone in a Mexican hotel room. Could he?

"What did she eat and drink?" the doctor asked. "Would you know that?"

The last thing Jamal needed at the moment was attitude from an old Mexican doctor.

"She had a Cuba Libre and some tacos. She hasn't touched

a thing since then. That was like forty-eight hours ago."

"What kind of tacos?"

"Veggie. She's a vegan."

"Then you know that much about her." Even the old doctor knew that much about her from his examination. "I am going to give you a note for three powerful medications, with instructions. Do you understand?"

"Three?" It seemed a lot.

"You must go to the Farmacias."

"Me? Why not you?"

"Will you accept any responsibility for this poor girl?"

Jamal dropped his head. The doctor shamed him like a father. Jamal got back on his phone, looking for the nearest drug store.

"Okay, I'm on it."

"She will sleep now, but you must do this right away. My fee will be on your hotel bill. If she takes a turn for the worse, call the front desk and they will call me. By this evening you must get her to eat some white rice."

"A turn for the worse? What's the worst?"

The doctor did not answer. Instead, he wrote a long note in Spanish and gave it to him, something for the pharmacist, whose work can often be boring.

47

Touristas, My Foot

"YOU WERE, LIKE, mega-sick," Jamal said.

"I know, right?"

She was much better now, sitting up in bed and eating white rice, one little bite at a time. He could at last relax. They would get back to San Francisco as scheduled. The romantic getaway had been a disaster, but they could laugh about it now.

"I had to chase all over Oaxaca trying to get your medicine, and everywhere I went I saw skulls and skeletons in the windows. It freaked me out."

She was sipping on a liter of the green fluid he had bought.

In the taxi he used his phone translator app to tell the driver to get him to the closest farmacia. He used it again to tell the pharmacist why he was there, handing him the note the doctor gave him. The pharmacist read the note and looked at him in an odd way.

"It's okay?"

The pharmacist spoke to him in Spanish. Together they worked the phone but it took too long and was giving them impossible translations.

"*Problema?*" Jamal asked.

"No," said the pharmacist, "*pero no tengo...solo tengo una...*"

"Una what?"

"De las cosas."

"But you're a drugstore. You're supposed to have the drugs, dude. Jesus!"

The pharmacist looked at him blankly.

He left with the three liters of colored fluids and flagged another taxi. He made this one wait for him after they found another farmacia. Jamal ran inside and pleaded, "*S'il vous plait, avez-vous...*" before he realized he was calling on his college French. He struggled to say, "*Tengo tu* these *cosas?*" The pharmacist read his note, looked into his plastic bag from the previous farmacia, and made him understand that he had one of the remaining items but not the other. Jamal wanted to weep and sleep.

He had brought enough rice back to the room so that he had some for himself, afraid now to eat anything else after seeing what happened to her.

"I had to jump back in the taxi and find a third farmacia and go through the whole routine again. By the time I got the all the stuff I was speaking Spanish I didn't know I had."

"Living in California, baby, you pick it up."

"The last dude smiled at me like I was an idiot. He stuck the note in his pocket, like he was the end of a scavenger hunt, which he was. I finally had three bags full of stuff. I told the driver to step on it. I was sure you'd die here. You were turning yellow! The soles of your feet were all yellow and orange!"

"They still are," she said.

"They are?"

"It's called carotenemia. It's from eating nothing but vegetables. It's not a big deal."

"But the doctor...? All those medicines."

"This stuff? Electrolytes. You give it to babies." She looked at the two boxes of pills. "This one's aspirin, for the fever. The other is antibiotics. I'm not going to take those. It was just a bad case of the *touristas*. By tomorrow I'll be fine. It could have been the ice in the Cuba Libre, or maybe there was lard in those tacos. God!"

He didn't want to think about it anymore or say anything more about his heroics in getting the remedies to save her life. Some doctor.

Now that she felt better, she took the whole thing lightly. Jamal looked stricken.

She said, "Mexico will still be here. We can come back."

"Sure," he said. "We can do that."

They did, but not with each other.

48

Don't Shoot

AS POLICE SHOOTINGS go, this one was different. The victim was white, with no police record, in the safety of his own home.

It began with a rookie telemarketer gesturing wildly to her Supervisor, who believed that the girl dressed inappropriately and was given to unnecessary anxieties.

"Now what?" the Supervisor said as she approached what's-her-name.

The young telemarketer was gasping for breath.

"I was talking to a man, and he told me to hold on...someone was at the door...and then I heard a shot...and he didn't come back to the phone..."

"Hang up," the Supervisor told her. "Make the next call."

"But...but...something terrible has happened. Shouldn't we call the police?"

"Hang up. People mess with us all the time. Get back to work."

What's-her-name made the next call, and the Supervisor was satisfied she was back on track, but the girl could not go on as though nothing had happened. Though she hated the job, she needed it desperately. Still, she did not want to hate the job and herself as well. She called 9-1-1 and reported the gun shot, the name and number and address of the man. Vincent Poteet of Reno, Nevada.

In fact, the Supervisor had it right. Vince had a gun—in Nevada everyone did—and was positioning it into his mouth when the phone rang. Vince despised telemarketers as much as everybody else did but he saw this call as an omen, a sign that he should go on living.

One might imagine a new affection for telemarketers, but that was not the case. He told her to hang on, there was someone at the door, and then he fired a shot into the sofa and laughed into his sleeve. He left the phone off the hook.

Two local cops were sent to the address, The Riverside Artists Lofts on Virginia, subsidized housing for struggling artists. One of the cops knocked on the door with his baton but no one answered. They ordered the Manager to open the door. He was reluctant but they were the *placa*, after all, and the manager was undocumented.

Inside, they called out, identifying themselves as R.P.D. They saw an easel set up in the studio area. A painting was in progress. It looked like a bridge in heavy fog. Music was coming from the bathroom, the door of which was closed. A light could be seen underneath it. The cops drew their Glocks and knocked on the door as they opened it.

Vince was in the bathtub, and the gun, forgotten now that he wasn't going to use it, sat on the edge of the tub. He was stoned, his eyes closed and his lips seeking out the roach, which he held aloft clamped in a tweezer. The cops shot him, seven times. The bathwater turned blood red.

At the hearing, the cops, one a ten-year veteran, the other having served three years, backed up each other's story: the victim was going for the gun.

The manager saw it differently. He saw the limp wrist naturally fall to the outside of the tub, as sometimes happens when you're stoned and have been too long in a hot bath. The cops were found to have acted appropriately. The young telemarketer was fired. The manager was deported.

49

Horses, Not Zebras

WATER FEATURES ARE popular in the landscape around desert homes. When it is 115 degrees in the shade it is soothing to hear water spill over rocks and into a pool.

When Harry bought a home in Old Las Palmas large enough for the children to visit with the grandchildren, he decided that a simple fountain didn't cut it. He envisioned a waterfall outside the master bedroom.

Will Roberts was the man everyone recommended for the job, and during the three months it took to construct the waterfall, using boulders trucked in from Colorado and placed by crane into a design created by Will and approved by Harry, they became pals, as much as contractors can be friends with clients. Many wind up in court.

Harry wanted lush lawns to surround the falls, to remind him of Michigan. Will talked him into sticking with desert landscaping, a few Mexican blue palm trees surrounded by upright rosemary and some butterfly iris. Lush enough in an endless drought.

The big day arrived. The falls were complete, waiting only for the water to be turned on. Will invited Harry to press the button. For an agonizing twenty seconds nothing happened. Then a rumble was heard and finally a burst of water spewed up from the top and cascaded over the boulders and into the pool. It was glorious.

They popped a bottle of champagne. Will walked Harry and Louise through the computerized operation, explaining how to set the timer and volume of flow. Harry nodded and declared he knew all he needed to know. The waterfall would go full tilt, twenty-four/seven. The wealthy retired couple could not have been happier with their waterfall. True, in the beginning it was difficult to sleep with the sound of it outside the bedroom, but they soon adjusted. After several days they could not imagine sleeping without that comforting sound.

By mid-May the snowbirds migrated back to Canada, Minnesota, Seattle, and points north, but Harry and Louise stayed on, year-rounders now.

Before Flag Day, Will went to the Eisenhower Medical Center to have his yearly physical, and in the waiting room was Harry, looking despondent. Will assumed they would be summering somewhere cooler. They greeted each other like friends and sat together. Harry told Will he was there to have a cystoscope, which is an invasive, uncomfortable, and humiliating look into the bladder.

"Doc said he might have to cut some of the prostate away. Could be something worse. I'll be honest with you, I'm a little scared."

"What are your symptoms?" asked Will.

"I'm up ten times a night to pee. It's murder."

"You still have that waterfall going twenty-four hours a day?"

"Absolutely. Everyone loves it. You did a great job."

"Go home. Right now. Reschedule your cystoscope for next week. Turn off the waterfall. Keep it off all week and give me a call."

Doctors have a saying: "When you hear the sound of hoof-beats, you think horses, not zebras."

Or for that matter, waterfalls.

50

Pre-Boarding

THEY PASSED EACH other at Gate 31. A little boy of ten with his parents and younger sister were going in one direction, and a man of forty was going in the other. They were walking toward different gates to board different planes to different cities.

The little girl pulled behind her a tiny carryon shaped like a miniature panda bear, and she was dressed in little girl clothes.

The little boy and the passing grown man, however, were wearing the same outfit: cargo shorts and shower shoes, T-shirts and backwards baseball caps, backpacks and ear buds.

They noticed each other in passing. Startled, the man quickened his pace. The boy turned and looked back over his shoulder. He was confused, as little boys often are by the adults they encounter in public places.

51

In the Absence Of

THE BOYS WERE too young to drive and so they waited at the bus stop after the mall closed, standing around or sitting on the bench, smoking cigarettes. They talked about how great it will be once they get their drivers' licenses. One of them, the group contrarian, argued against getting a license, against having to buy insurance and suffering a stupid job to bear the expense of a car. Tim was not that boy, but it made him think. He took a drag on his cigarette and practiced his French inhale.

A car half-way down the street started up and slowly rolled toward them, illuminating them in its headlights. Tim recognized the car and dropped his cigarette. He turned away from the lights. The car stopped in the bus zone. The passenger's window came down.

Two men were in the car, big men with menacing faces, which would be the only way the teen-agers could describe them to kids at school the next day. They thought they looked like hitmen. One of them was older than the other and the younger man was bald by choice, his arms and neck heavily inked, making him appear even scarier. The men stared at them. The kid who didn't want a driver's license said with admirable bravado, "Can we *help* you?"

The passenger, the older man, said one word: "Tim."

Tim turned around but did not speak. The man crooked his finger and Tim went to the open window and leaned down. The others shrunk back.

"Was it eleven you were supposed to get on the bus?" the man said, in a voice that was low and threatening.

"No, sir."

"What was it, then?"

"It was when I was supposed to be home."

"Then what are you doing here?"

"We missed the bus."

"Gave you time to smoke a cigarette," said the driver.

"I'm sorry."

"You're sorry? We're disappointed. And pissed. You smoke at fifteen, you'll be smoking for the next ten years, maybe the rest of your life. Damage done. How are we going to feel about that?"

"Dunno."

"We're not going for stupid here, we want you to be smart," said the driver.

"I am smart," Tim said, but he was never sure. He got good grades.

"Get in the car."

Tim looked at his friends. He could not hide his embarrassment. He got into the back seat. The car drove away.

The next morning at school the same kids plus some who were not there the night before gathered around Tim when he arrived. They asked what happened. They conjectured that the men were either gangsters or narcs. They were about to dial 9-1-1 if Tim didn't show up for school.

Tim, who was not known as a bad-ass, noticed his friends had a new respect for him. He smiled and let them answer their own questions.

52

Dumar the Dog

FRANK HUNG HIS helmet on the mirror, stretched out the kinks in his body, and walked into the bar called The Elbow Room. He was on his way home, Fourth of July. He wanted a beer and to think over if he had another hundred miles riding the Harley left in him.

An older couple was at one end of the bar talking to the barmaid, and at the other end, a Mexican picker drinking to forget. Frank noticed a scruffy dog lying under the pool table. A mongrel. He clucked and when the old dog came to him patted his grey head. He would swear the dog smiled at him before returning to his spot.

Ten minutes later a cowboy came down the hall from the back door into the bar proper. You could hear his boot-falls, like trouble coming for somebody. The bar maid nodded toward the mongrel and said, "He's under the pool table." Frank watched the cowboy in the mirror through the whiskey bottles take off his sweat-stained hat and swat the old dog. He grabbed the animal by his collar and pulled him away. A moment of embarrassed silence followed.

"You can't blame Dumar," said the bar maid.

"Who is Dumar?" Frank asked.

They told Frank the story. Dumar belonged to Sandy, a

woman who used to work behind the bar. The dog used to come to work with her. He loved the general bonhomie and the considerate way people treated dogs they happened to find in a bar. When Sandy took up with Cecil, a self-styled cowboy, she quit her job. Dumar must not have liked her taste in men. He would trot off to the bar whenever the new boyfriend came home.

"That poor dog has no idea why that cowboy came in and swatted him," said Frank.

"He should know by now. Happens often enough."

"Too bad. Don't you feel sorry for old Dumar?"

"Sure. We let him in but then we have to call Cecil. Another beer?"

Frank declined. Whatever the sense of failure, loss or cheerless witness that was triggered by the old dog being dragged away, one more beer would not serve to diminish.

"A dog like that looks like a sweet companion," Frank said. "I would like a dog like that."

"Dumar's getting up in years."

"So am I," said Frank. "Where's this Sandy live?"

* * *

The cowboy came out of the single-wide, holding a sweating bottle of Corona, alerted by the rumble of the Harley. A jerry-built raised porch led to the front door. He stood behind the railing.

Dumar, chained to a doghouse outside, got to his paws. Frank swore he saw the glint of recognition in the dog's eyes and maybe a look of hope. He also realized Dumar might be larger than first he thought.

Frank cut the engine, put down the kickstand, and dismounted. He put his helmet on the mirror.

"Cecil? Who's out there?" Frank assumed that would be Sandy.

"Damned if I know. Some retired accountant on a Harley."

He was not far from wrong.

Sandy came out and asked him what he wanted. She had seen some desperate days.

"Evening, miss. I would like you to give me that dog over there."

"Dumar? I ain't giving you my dog. Who the hell are you?"

"Well, maybe a dog rescuer, I don't know. I'll give you a hundred dollars for him."

"Sell the mutt," said the cowboy. "I'm gonna have to put him down soon enough anyway."

"He's got some time left. I had him since he was a pup," Sandy said.

She fussed over the offer half-heartedly. She either could not refute the cowboy's reasoning, or she lived in fear of him. She agreed to the deal.

"Thing is, I don't have the hundred on me," said Frank. "Over and above gas money, I got ten. I can mail you the rest." He turned his eyes to Cecil. "And that's about all the accounting I know."

"Hit the road, dirtbag," said the cowboy, leaning on his forearms against the stoop rail.

Frank had to jump up to land the punch, like a goalie after a soccer ball. It landed right on the button. The cowboy's nose spurted blood. After the shock of looking at his own hand full of blood, Cecil jumped over the rail and onto Frank's head. Frank did okay, but he was no match. Cecil had weight behind him while Frank was burdened with the years.

Sandy helped her bleeding boyfriend back inside to repair the damage, leaving the stranger unconscious.

From his horizontal place in the dirt, Frank came to and inventoried what hurt. Pretty much everything, inside and out. He turned his head and came eye to eye again with Dumar, who had returned to his down position, chin on crossed paws,

127

looking sorry for him.

Frank thought, there are two kinds of dogs in the world: those that like to ride on motorcycles and those who...oh, hell, they *all* like to ride on motorcycles.

Cecil and Sandy slept through the parade but got up in time to join the celebration at the park, where they drank and later watched the fireworks. When they finally returned to the trailer, drunk for the second night in a row, a little worse than the first, they did not notice that Dumar was gone.

While they were sleeping it off the previous night, Dumar was enjoying the ride, sitting snug up against Frank's belly, paws braced on the gas tank, wind into his open mouth and puffing up his cheeks, bound for his new home.

By the time Sandy and Cecil got around to noticing that Dumar was missing, they blamed his disappearance on the fireworks. Dogs always go missing after fireworks. Cecil told her Dumar would show up eventually, but he never did.

53

Outside of the Cake

WHEN HE WAS living in Los Angeles, Owen became friends with another writer, this one famous. They often lunched together at Cantor's delicatessen. His name was Carlos Castaneda. His critics accused him of writing fiction, but he insisted he was an anthropologist.

"The world is already here," he told Owen. "It is done. It can be described in all its changes and toyed with, but it's already invented. You should hear this old Mexican woman I have on tape talk about her life. A novelist of great genius could not come close to her, and she has never gone fifty miles from her village."

"Fiction writing is a re-creation," Owen said. "If I heard the old woman, I could re-create her words within the context of a story, for a specific effect."

Carlos seemed not to have much of an idea what fiction was or how it was made. Or care.

"Novelist or scholar, one way or another we're all faking it," said Owen.

Carlos laughed in his robust way and told Owen of an experience he had that was still playing out.

"I heard that some professor was giving a traveling lecture, on *me*, at different places around Los Angeles, wherever he could find a vacant hall. He was charging four dollars to attend. He presented himself as an expert with impeccable credentials. His name was Udo Kullechenski. That drove me up the wall! Did you ever in your life hear of anybody named Udo? He'd been educated in all the academic capitals of Europe and now was an expert on *me*. Annie and I went to hear him in Torrance. I had already gone to a couple of his lectures, but I wanted Annie to hear it. We slipped into the last row and out comes Udo, elbow patches on his jacket, a look of utter contempt on his face, a person who judges people immediately upon first glance. He'd look at you and say, 'You're an idiot.' A perfect professor!"

"Did he accuse you of writing fiction?"

"Not exactly. He took a balanced point of view. He had a slide projector that flashed those pictures from my interview in *Time*. Udo had read all the books and all the articles and all the reviews and, as I said, was an expert on the subject. Me! During the question-and-answer period I stood up and asked, "Have you ever met Carlos Castaneda, sir?"

"'Well, no,' he said. 'No one *meets* Castaneda. How can one? He lives in the shadows, with no address or phone. He has a small inner circle sworn to secrecy. He is reclusive to the extreme.' I shouted, 'Well, I think he is a fake! He could work at Taco Bell, for all you know. He could be in this room with his family, chuckling at your lecture.'"

Carlos had indeed worked at Taco Bell, under an alias, and he was in the room with Annie who counted as family, and they were chuckling.

"Some in the audience were offended. They told me to sit down."

"Was Udo offended?" asked Owen.

"On the one hand, he was. On the other, he defended me. Thank God he didn't have a third hand!"

They were sitting in a corner booth and Carlos had ordered a pastrami on rye bread. With his fingers, he ate the meat and bread separately, as was his habit. He ordered coffee and dessert, but he took, again as was his habit, exactly one sip of the coffee and only one bite of the dessert. His object of study who had become his mentor, a desert sorcerer called Don Juan, had instructed him to practice that as part of his diet. He did not explain why. On this day, dessert was carrot cake. After his single bite Carlos said, disappointed, "No nuts." His smile was impish. "Maybe there are enough nuts outside of the cake."

54

My Year of Serious Drinking

OWEN HAD HAD better ideas for books, but he was sick of writing novels no one wanted to read. He would prefer this time that *everyone* read his book and have a good time and make him rich and famous. On Amazon he scanned the genres of books that did that for their authors, most of them by women, for women.

A sub-genre of non-fiction books became evident, the "Year" books. The author would set out to do something extraordinary for a year, record the process, and publish the results to good reception. Most of these books, too, seemed to be written by women for women, but not all of them. Some of them were written by men for women. He could break the mold if he did something for a year that he could write about for men, and maybe for a particular kind of woman, the kind he knew well.

He had never published nonfiction, nor focused on a challenge that was marked by the duration of one year, not even the writing of his novels which generally took twice that long. Still, there had to be something he could do, something like but unlike, (A Year...) in Provence, Down Under, by the Sea, Without Makeup, of Biblical Womanhood, of Miracles, of Living Peacefully, of Reading Dangerously, of Magical Thinking..., all of which sounded fascinating and one or two of which he might have to read to get the technique down.

Within the "Year" books he discovered a sub-sub-genre that appealed to him: doing something dangerously.

A movie he enjoyed, "Julia and Julia", was based on a book by a woman who cooked every meal in the Julia Childs cookbook during the course of one year. It was called "My Year of Cooking Dangerously." He could do something like that. Take a well-known book, digest it, so to speak, and regurgitate it in a more entertaining form.

But what? He pondered the possibilities over a perfect Manhattan at Melvyn's. Clive had the skill to eyeball the mix and then pour everything out of the shaker to fill a glass to the brim, forcing Owen to lean over and take the first couple of sips without using his hands, like an alcoholic with the shakes. The idea landed on him, as they sometimes did after half a Manhattan. He could make a non-fiction book out of drinking every cocktail in "Mr. Boston: Official Bartender's and Party Guide." He would do it over the course of one year. A dangerous year.

After the third cocktail Owen called a cab to get him back home. His enthusiasm for the new project caught fire. A sure success, an invitation to appear on Fresh Air and be interviewed by Terry Gross. "Thanks for having me, cheers," he would sign off. Technically, he had already begun the project at Melvyn's, but he wouldn't count that. It was imperative he start with the first drink in the book and have them all in order. He couldn't wait to get home.

The first four drinks listed, however, required ingredients he did not possess, things like blackberry flavored brandy, champagne, Triple Sec, Creme d Cacao, vanilla beans...

He sat with his feet up, composing in his mind the preface. It would be forgotten by morning. The preface, not the idea.

55

Our Undertaker

THEIR FRIEND DIGGER drifted away from the gang as they grew older. Maybe because Digger became a professional and they were just working stiffs or looking-for-work stiffs. They took pride in Digger's accomplishments, even if his position was passed down from his father. When they were younger, they enjoyed introducing him to strangers, especially when they were trying to pick up girls in bars. "My name is Eddie. This is Gi-Gi and Joey and Chewie. And this is Digger, our undertaker."

Now retired, what was left of the gang played cribbage in their favorite booth in their favorite bar, remembering those nights from their youth. They were long past trying to pick up girls.

"The girls thought it was a joke because Digger had this hangdog look about him. Remember?"

"Sad Sack."

"He was."

"And all the undertakers were old back then."

"Everybody was old back then, cops and priests and whatnot."

"Except for us."

"And now we caught up."

"Fifteen-two, fifteen-four, shut the door," Gi-Gi counted up his score.

Eddie said, "Nobody thinks it's funny when you're at a party and you introduce Jim, your accountant, or Mike, your lawyer."

"You have an accountant, a lawyer?"

"I'm just saying."

They had no need of accountants or lawyers, and didn't have any as friends, and wouldn't be invited to those kinds of parties anyway.

"It is kind of funny. Meet my undertaker."

"When Digger got into the family business," said Eddie, "I promised him he would get the job when my time came."

"He's still waiting."

"He appreciated it because, you know, I'm Catholic and all."

"He always looked sad, Digger did."

"You'd look sad, too, if you was a Protestant undertaker in a Catholic town."

"True that. He'll never get rich."

"The Catholic undertakers all drive Cadillacs."

"Like the priests…"

"The ministers drive Chevys."

"Do Protestants take a vow of poverty?"

That struck them as funny.

"Protestants eat fish on Fridays."

Even funnier.

"Do you think they just hang around waiting for people to die?"

"Protestants?"

"Undertakers."

"Ask Digger."

56

As L'il Kim Would Say

ONE OF THE three men who held up the 7-Eleven had a gun. The plan was that it should be used as a fear factor only. The least experienced of the three drove the car and acted as a lookout, though he wore glasses and had already wrecked two cars, neither of which was his own. The unarmed thief guarded the door from the inside while the one with the gun pointed it sideways at the turbaned head of the clerk and demanded the money.

By some gesture or word never made clear at the trial, the clerk was disrespectful, so the gunman shot him in the face. The unarmed one screamed a lot of oh, shit, why? why? why? while the gunman gathered up as much cash as he could.

On hearing the shot, the frightened driver sped away and wrecked the car. When arrested he waived his right to have a lawyer present. He answered every question put to him.

Outside the 7-Eleven, looking for their getaway car, the distraught unarmed thief could not believe how badly things had gone wrong and moaned regretful sounds.

The gunman said, "It is what it is." Sentenced to life without the possibility of parole, he said, "It's all good."

57

Bent

THE FIRST OPENLY gay mayor in the city's history was handsome, poised, optimistic, cheerful and popular. The few criticisms made of him were pushed back and seen as homophobic by the gay community, a political force in the city.

By all accounts he was good for business, which in most cities forgives everything else. He won re-election in a landslide. A small group of longtime residents, however, believed he was allowing real estate development to get out of hand in an effort to attract more tourists to spend money and perhaps buy second homes, which they could then rent out short-term when they were not using them, providing a cash flow of Transient Occupancy Tax to the city. This element of the new economy led to raucous parties at night in what used to be quiet neighborhoods. By day, residents suffered the noise of endless construction and the unpredictable roar of leaf blowers raising toxic clouds of dust. Tests found that the asthma rate had significantly increased.

It was accepted as the price of progress by the mayor's supporters.

Every Friday a group of fifteen retired gay men met for coffee and talk. They were proud that one of their own was a popular mayor, but a vocal few expressed emerging misgivings.

The mayor had arranged half-million-dollar grants to two upscale restaurants for refurbishing. One of them raised the price of their best steak to ninety dollars and charged twenty dollars for a four-ounce pour of the house red. The other restaurant hosted swim parties with a D.J., making weekends almost unbearable for neighborhood residents. The majority of the Friday group, however, still stood with the mayor, believing the investment would pay off in the long run and make the city an even better place in which to live.

The discussions did not become heated until the FBI raided city hall and it was revealed that the mayor was on the payroll of a developer as a "consultant," for two hundred thousand dollars a year. This developer also happened to be the owner of that restaurant with the loud DJ, which was now being sued by several sub-contractors and was headed for bankruptcy, voiding the generous city loan that made the business possible.

Though the mayor called all accusations against him politically motivated and homophobic, he quit his consulting job to eliminate any hint of impropriety.

Even then the mayor had his defenders within the discussion group, but they were fewer with each new damning revelation.

As a group, they were noticeably depressed. During a sad lull in the discourse, one of them said, "Just because he's gay doesn't mean he's straight."

58

Sunday, Sunday

ON MONDAY, OWEN and Carlos were back at Cantor's deli for lunch. Carlos took apart his sandwich and ate its parts in sequence.

Owen said, "In your book, remember Don Juan's description of life?"

"How could I forget it? He describes it like an ordinary Sunday at home! Life. Like a Sunday at home."

"Yeah, reading the papers, watching the game, family dinner, maybe a little nap. Comfortable enough. A little on the warm side. Nothing to do, kind of boring, but okay. And soon night falls. That rattled me. 'And soon night falls.'"

"Me, too!" Carlos said in mock horror. He was the only man Owen knew who spoke in exclamation points. "Of all the metaphors for life, why did he have to choose the one that would scare me the most? Sunday! That's the day I get to relax."

Owen's marriage was unraveling. He wanted to talk to Carlos about it, but Carlos trivialized traditional institutions like marriage and the self-inflicted pain that ensues. He asked after June, though, and that provided an opening.

"She's fine. We're both fine, individually but not together."

"I saw that, last time I was at your house."

"You did? I don't know how to be with her anymore. It's

painful."

"It's a real problem," Carlos said. "With my ward, I never know when I am infringing on her time and privacy or if I've said the wrong thing or if I'm in her way."

"Your ward? You have a ward?"

"Oh, boy, do I have a ward! Annie. I thought you knew."

"Wait, what? Annie is your *ward*? Annie with the black belt in karate?"

"That's the one."

Carlos explained how it came to be. He had a sweater to which he was attached, made in Denmark, with all sorts of zippers and pockets.

"You couldn't get it off me. That sweater and my ripple-soled shoes were my uniform. One night I forgot it and left it hanging over at Annie's place. Next day, on my way to Mexico I stopped to pick it up because I would not travel without it. As soon as I arrived at Don Juan's casita, he started circling me and sniffing, like a coyote. He grabbed my arm and sniffed hard at the sweater. He was excited and said, 'What is this?' I said I didn't know what scent he was picking up unless it was Annie's apartment or Annie herself. 'You must take care of this girl,' he said, like it was the most important thing in the universe. 'How?' I asked. 'How should I know?' he said. Later, when I brought her down to Mexico and he met her, he reconfirmed what he had told me. It was my destiny to look after Annie."

"For how long?"

"For life! That's what destiny means!"

Owen tried to make sense of it. "She does have an odd element of vulnerability, but she can clearly take care of herself."

"She could eat me alive! I ought to be *her* ward!"

Owen never pried into Carlos's relationships, but he had to ask. He had always believed Carlos to be celibate, that sex would be a distraction to his work.

"Is she your lover?"

"She is everything in life. My friend, my colleague, my sister, everything. Ultimately, thanks to Don Juan, she is my ward. Do you see?"

"Not really."

"Me neither! Look, you can drop me anywhere. Drop me in a remote village in China and I'll get along. I'm a hustler in that way. But I am the least qualified person in the world to take care of anyone, especially someone like Annie."

"Then why did Don Juan…"

He clenched his fists on the deli table. "I don't know! He creates these hopeless situations and watches me squirm."

He ordered a cup of coffee and a piece of apple pie. He took one bite of pie followed by one sip of coffee.

"But we were talking about you," said Carlos. "You should go away," he told Owen. "For six months. Alone."

"Why?"

"You know why."

"So I won't be here when it all crumbles and dies?"

"You won't be the villain. She'll thank you when you return. If you return! Remove yourself from the scenario. Go and don't let anyone know where you are."

"Go where?

"Caracas."

Owen laughed. "Why six months?"

"Okay, seven months."

"Why Caracas, of all places?"

"Exactly!"

Owen did go to Caracas and told no one, but he lasted only six weeks, not six months. He met a young woman there, an American, but nothing happened between them. She was escaping something as well. By the time he returned, Carlos and Annie had disappeared and his marriage had ended.

59

Loaded

IT HAPPENS TO everybody, is what Harry told himself as he drove to Brady's place. It's normal. People misplace things. A loaded shotgun can be misplaced like a corduroy jacket you haven't worn in a couple years.

He did find it finally, upright in his closet between two black, pin-striped suits, neither of which had seen any action since the shotgun itself had. At the time he did not know if it was loaded and ready to fire. He assumed it was not, because Johnny Cash once stated that nothing scares a bad guy more than that distinctive sound of a shell being pumped into the chamber of a shotgun. Harry took that advice to heart. In the matter of a revolver, Willie Nelson advised keeping the first chamber empty, so you would have to pull the trigger twice if you meant business.

Relieved at finding his home protection again, Harry pumped it to see if it was loaded, and in that instant it became so. He was alarmed to see a shell rise up from the bowels of the piece and nestle into the chamber. Now what? He tried to pump it again, but nothing moved. The weapon had a safety, but he could not determine whether it was off or on. The red dot told him nothing. He did recall once clearing out the shells without firing the shotgun. What he could not remember now was how he did it. He would have to take the shotgun to Brady at his place of business.

Harry worried that he should not be driving around the city with a loaded shotgun in his car.

Brady had seen combat, unlike Harry who served his part of the Vietnam war in Fort Dix. We attribute a greater knowledge of weaponry to combat veterans than they have. Brady had no clue how to clear the shotgun. The best he could do was invite Harry to go over to his loading dock and pull the trigger. Harry took aim at a gnarly bush growing out of the melting macadam. The sound of the report was loud enough to add tinnitus to Harry's growing list of medical complaints. Brady wondered aloud if someone might call the cops.

Harry returned home with the still loaded, now hot, shotgun in the trunk of his car.

Another friend of Harry's, Roger, lived in Montana off the grid, except for his membership in the NRA. They were on opposite ends of the political spectrum but stayed in sporadic touch. Harry called him and told him of his problem. "I've tried everything," he said. "There's no way to unload this bitch."

"*Au contraire, mon frere*," Roger said, ironically, because he despised the French. He knew that Harry, on the other hand, loved all things French, beginning with the pouty girls. It was one more thing the two friends did not have in common.

Roger directed him to a metal toggle hidden below the stock. Once moved, it allowed him to work the pump and empty the weapon. He replaced the weapon between the two black suits he never wore, but this time he wrote a Post-It to remind himself of the hiding place. He stuck the Post-It on his bookcase, out of view behind some first editions. He thought he might forget the shotgun's hiding place but was confident he would remember the Post-It. That confidence proved to be unfounded.

60

Just a Vacation

THE SCREENWRITER, WHO unaccountably lived in Reno, was valued highly enough by the producer to be transported to LAX by limo. The screenwriter did not know that the producer was *this* project away from living in his car. Had he known he would have taken the bus.

He got into the car at Paramount and before they got past the gate the driver was pitching his own script, a time travel adventure gag, "Back to the Future" meets "The Wild Bunch." The screenwriter begged off, explaining that he was himself struggling to gain a foothold and couldn't get an agent for anyone. He would be lucky to hold onto his own.

At that point he became dead to the driver.

Half the seatbelt was stuck under the seat. The screenwriter dug in for it while the limo picked up more than enough speed. His hand fell on something hard, deep into the crack between the seat and the backrest. He pulled out a blue Tiffany bag with a drawstring. Inside was the famous jewelry line's version of a Swiss Army knife.

It had a corkscrew, an awl, an eye hook, a small regular screwdriver, and a micro screwdriver, all on one side. On the other side: a pair of scissors, a can opener (with another small screwdriver), a bottle opener (with a larger screwdriver), a pair of pliers, a magnifying glass, a saw, a file, a Phillips screwdriver, a fish scaler, and two actual knife blades (one two and a half inches and the other half that long). But wait, there's more. In hidden slots: a toothpick, a pair of tweezers, and a nail. Not to mention some decorative work on each side. It was a wonder of design, utility and construction.

It had to be worth hundreds. It was Tiffany after all. His impulse was to give it to the driver, but he was sure the driver would keep it. Who knows how many passengers have come and gone since someone lost it. It might have come out of the pocket of some A-list actor on his way to a film location. Or maybe some rich woman had it in her purse and realized it would be confiscated by airport security. (She could retrieve it later by requesting the same car.) Or maybe it was put there deliberately to get rid of it because it was linked to a crime.

The Trial of the Century was underway, in which the only missing evidence was the murder weapon. The prosecution's theory was that O.J., the accused, took a limo to the airport that night and dumped the knife into an airport trash barrel. That made more sense than stashing it in a limo. The murder weapon would have sealed the deal, but they had plenty of other evidence. He examined again the Tiffany knife. It was designed for any eventuality save murder, but who knows? O.J. may not have had murder on his mind, but he did have a weapon in his pocket.

The screenwriter dropped the silver knife into his shoulder bag. It was the only thing he ever owned from Tiffany's.

O.J. was found not guilty.

The night of the verdict he sat next to an older black woman at the blackjack table. He asked her what she thought about the whole thing.

She said, "Just a vacation, baby." At least that's what he thought she said.

61

Trolling

STEWART WAS AT the till of his Boston Whaler. He looked like an old poet, with gray hair in the wind and beard gone wild, skin weathered and furrowed. He trolled for salmon just before the onset of high tide, using lures and flashers on one side of the boat and herrings and spinners on the other.

The fact that he *was* a poet would lead those who knew him to say he looked like a fisherman, but few knew him, and he preferred it that way.

Fishing stopped his thinking or freed it to go deeper. Either way.

He wanted a King, but a Coho would do. He would make gravlax out of it. From the catching to the consuming of it, gravlax is a week's effort. He would cure it and eat it with a dill sauce of his own making. His wife, Docia, did not care for gravlax. The old poet would eat as much of it as he could over a few cocktail hours and then sauté what was left for a sandwich.

In the doldrums of waiting for a rod tip to go down, he thought again about how a poem was like catching a fish. You know how it is done, but it's all in luring one to you. Often after hooking a good one, you lose it at the net. It slips away, and you regret its loss. Some are better than others and you don't know why. Immature ones you toss back. As time goes by you have to go further out and deeper down to catch one. It is a fight and where the joy is. Coming back into the bay you stand up in your boat and hold up your fish to show it off and sometimes people pretend to give a damn. No matter. You have done what you set out to do. You will feast on it.

The starboard rod dipped down and the old poet set the hook, killed the engine, and reeled in. He knew by its feel it was not a King. This fish was lazy, giving himself up too soon. He feared it was not a salmon at all, and he was right. It was a dogfish, universally held in contempt by all fishermen, some of whom kill them before throwing them back, or snap the line and make the dogfish live the rest of its life with a hook through its lip. No one eats them, not even other fish.

This dogfish was an ugly thing with nothing to commend it. Stewart reached overboard, keeping the fish on the surface of the water. He turned out the hook. The encounter meant more to the poet than to the dogfish, who took a moment to recover, then slowly finned down.

62

Slump

"HELA TIME TO lose my stuff," lamented the pitcher recently brought up from Triple-A.

The woman whose name he'd forgotten didn't say anything.

"Naw, gotta cut the negative thoughts. The next pitch is gonna be a strike. Always. Catch the corner, get him looking."

She nodded, as though trying to reassure him.

"Let's face it, yo, the slider isn't breaking. The cutter ain't fast enough. Last week I tried to throw a knuckle ball. Me. It hit the ground six feet in front of Buster and smacked the ump right in the face. Oh, God."

She hummed her sympathy.

"I can't go back to Fresno. I can't…I can't…I…Yes! Yes!"

He fell silent, except for his heavy breathing. He lay back and pictured a string of K's, up by the scoreboard. He would work out of this.

You can't underestimate encouragement from a loyal fan.

63

A Long Way to Tipperary

WHEN OWEN MET Doc Quaid at Melvyn's they hit it off right away. They were surprised they hadn't run into each other before that. Doc was curious, though, about why Owen would order a new drink every round. It seemed unnatural.

Owen finished a rye whiskey cocktail and Doc expected that he'd order another. Instead, he asked for a seaboard, followed by a shamrock, followed by a Swiss Family cocktail. He had in front of him now a T-Bird. Though Doc himself was a high functioning alcoholic, he was sober enough to notice that Owen's drinks were coming in alphabetical order.

For Owen's part, he was fascinated that during their time together at the bar that night Doc was called away twice to do a quick examination in the men's room. He asked Clive the bartender about it.

"Happens all the time," he said. "Mostly Doc puts someone's mind at ease, pro bono. Sometimes it's a serious thing, but mostly just rashes or odd lumps."

Owen was touched by that. Often at a doctor's office he felt that he was no more than a customer. When Doc returned from a consultation in the men's room, Owen complimented him on his altruism and easy availability. He also told him that he was not feeling all that well himself these days.

"What seems to be the problem?"

"Sour stomach, pain in the side, some dizziness."

Owen followed Doc down the narrow stairway to the men's room, a hand on each wall to steady himself. Doc pressed his hand against where Owen's liver ought to be. Owen felt the pain.

"How many drinks a day do you have?" inquired the doctor.

"Six, seven…eight. After my day's writing."

"Well, okay, you're a moderate drinker. But mixing your drinks like that is be playing havoc with your system."

"You think?"

"Don't you have a regular drink?"

Owen explained that he was drinking his way through "Mr. Boston's Official Bartender's and Party Guide," in one year in order to write a book about it. Doc made no judgements but did that "Hmmmm" thing that doctors do.

"The bourbon section was cool, but I gagged through the brandy section. I had no idea. I'm through the gin, rum, scotch, tequila, vodka…I'm finishing the whiskey section now."

Back upstairs, he ordered a TNT.

When the drink was served Doc asked, "What's a TNT?"

"Whiskey and anisette."

"The hell."

"I know."

"And you're writing about it?"

"Yeah. It's not a pretty story. I'm dreading cordials and liqueurs."

"How much more do you have to go?"

"I'm in the home stretch. Come December I'll be doing hot drinks, eggnogs, and punch. That'll be the hardest part. Who drinks hot booze? I've got to finish by year's end."

"You'll be dead before that. Just saying."

"Really?"

"My professional opinion."

Owen preferred to talk about other things then, the unique beauty of fall in the desert and such.

He ordered a Tipperary cocktail, and again Doc passed. He turned toward the piano player but turned back when Owen groaned.

"Chartreuse," he explained.

"Good lord. Do people still drink that?"

"Feels like I've been poisoned."

"By yourself. No one's forcing you."

Owen's head dropped to his chest. Doc patted him on the back the way you do when your friend drops out of his first half-marathon.

It would not be the first book Owen abandoned, nor the only one he ever cried over.

64

Paris, the Last Time

FRANK DIED IN Paris. His son, Guy, flew over from Philadelphia on the first flight he could book. His death was unexpected, from an aneurism described as, "*Aussi gros qu'un ballon de football*." Guy was a former place kicker for the Raiders. He knew the doctor was referring to a soccer ball.

He spent his time on the plane regretting that he had fallen out of touch with his father. When Frank told him that he would not be returning from his latest trip to Europe, he thought it somehow frivolous. He had to admit, though, that his father had reached that age where he had nothing for which to be responsible. Why not be frivolous?

The concierge let him into the apartment, which turned out to be an artist's garret, a cozy and creatively messy place. His father had been living a cliché.

Guy shuffled through dozens of sketches of nudes done in charcoal, ink, and conté. It looked like the same nude in each of them. They weren't half-bad, for someone with no training. He found a pack of Gauloises and a box of matches from a brasserie, *Le Sully*. Had his father taken up smoking? Nothing now would surprise him, he thought. But he underestimated his father.

He said his final tearless good-bye in the hospital's morgue and then spoke to the attending physician. Afterwards, he sat at

Rotunde in Montparnesse, a walk of several minutes from his father's garret, and called his mother. Though no longer married to Frank, his mother kept an interest in his well-being and now in the circumstances of his death. She had settled into thinking of him as a friend with whom she had once shared a hazardous journey, the end of which put them at different destinations.

"I was thinking of a cremation, bring his ashes home with me."

"Do what you think is best, dear," she told Guy.

"That's what I had in mind, but as it turns out, I don't have to make any decisions," he said, without telling her why. He talked instead about the garret, the sketches, the cigarettes, and, "Guess what? He had a tattoo. A bumblebee, which the doctor told me was Napoleon's symbol. On his inner thigh."

His mother thought that was too much. She laughed, trying to imagine it.

"No fool like an old fool," she said. "He got through the navy without a tattoo."

"Yeah. So, when I talked to this doctor…the aneurism opened up in the hospital as he was being tested. He was bleeding out internally. The doctor told him he could operate but the odds were not in his favor. Dad told him that he had just lived the best year of his life and it was a good time to go. He took a pass on surgery and died."

His mother said, "Hmmm…well."

"I asked him if Dad had any last words."

"Did he?"

"He did. Ready?"

"Oh, my. Go ahead."

"His last words: 'Bury me under Paris ground.'"

His mother was relieved.

"So that's what he wanted, that's what I'll do, but I'm not sure how to go about it. Right now, I've got to get some sleep. Then I'll try to get the hotel to help me."

"You're a good son."

"One more thing."

He paused for too long a time.

"Go ahead, Guy. It can't matter now."

"I'm with the doctor and I'm like, 'It's sad that he died alone, hearing voices in a different language.' I said that in my high school French and the doctor goes off in real French. I got most of it, but what I heard make no sense to me, so we found a translator."

"And?"

"Well, Dad didn't die alone. The doctor said his daughter was with him.'"

"What?"

"I know, right?"

"But you're an only child."

Guy would explain it to her when he got back to Philadelphia with his father's sketches. Or not.

65

Malta, the First Time

WHEN FRANK WAS a sailor with the Sixth Fleet, deployed in the Mediterranean, his ship was anchored for ten days at Malta, a liberty stop that only he, it seemed, enjoyed. His shipmates saw it as a rock, with no place to go and nothing to do. Frank found beauty in the stoney landscape and the changing colors and especially the people, who were a mix of all the cultures and races that had dominated the tiny island over the centuries. When Frank was there, it was the British, not known as a comely race, so time would tell.

He met a girl named Mary, a nurse, a dark exotic beauty different from any girl he had ever seen back home. She was lithe when she walked and shy when she talked, with a soft voice that made one calm. He met her in a neighborhood pub called The Green Lantern, where sailors usually did not go. She was there with a friend who had to leave early. Frank bought her a drink and she allowed him to sit at her table. They talked until close to midnight when he had to get back to the ship. She invited him to a picnic on the beach.

It was a Sunday and he had liberty all day. She took him to the beach by bus. Malta was crawling with loud rocking buses. It was how everyone got around.

The beach was not sand but tiny pebbles. Mary spread out

a blanket and served him a picnic of a small sandwich with one slice of ham on buttered bread, followed by a pear. Both were delicious. He ate the pear to the core and then looked for a place to toss it. Mary was still eating hers, in a different way. He watched her make the most of that little pear. She pulled at the core with the unpolished nails of her slender fingers, removing all of the fruit until nothing was left but the stem and some seeds, which she buried in a little hole she made under the pebbles.

Fifty years later he read that the amount of food wasted in America would fill the Rose Bowl on a daily basis.

Ever after, Frank himself wasted no food. As he grew older, he wasted neither water nor gas nor electricity nor paper nor even words.

Some women, he noticed, would order a three-course meal and have only one bite of each course. It was said to be healthier not to finish everything on one's plate. Frank not only finished everything on his plate, he finished whatever was left on his wife's plate.

Kiran, his wife, said his admonishments were long past their usefulness. He told her, "Chinese children really were going hungry when I was a kid. Now American children are going hungry."

He finished everything on his plate. He would not let the refrigerator door stay open for longer than necessary. He still took Navy showers. If he didn't need the whole page, he tore it in half. He never threw away a rubber band or a paper clip.

His family thought he was frugal to a fault. He would not be able to take it with him, etcetera. Some said his thrift was likely the result of being a Depression baby of financially traumatized parents.

No, all that he knew about not wasting was learned watching Mary eat a pear at a picnic on the beach in Malta.

66

Fish Fry

GI-GI AND JOEY thought Eddie had cancer and wasn't telling anyone. That might be an explanation for his recent odd behavior. First, out of the blue, this switch to fancy drinks—at the moment, they were having Kentucky cocktails—and then all this mooning about Chewie and the past. None of them had anything to do with that except they were there at the time.

When Eddie went to the head Gi-Gi whispered, "It might be PTS."

"Please." said Joey. "Are you all PTSed over a barroom fight forty-some years ago? Neither am I. Eddie has a Purple Heart, for crissake, he's not PTS."

"Then why's he digging all that shit up again?"

When Eddie returned, he did appear haunted by it.

"Listen," Joey said, "everybody felt bad, okay? Chewie was a good kid."

"We went ahead the next day," said Eddie, "and had the fish fry. How could we do that?"

"Chas had all those trout he caught. They would of gone to waste."

"I can still hear him," said Eddie. "Holding his gut in…"

"Shake it off, man."

"…and saying, 'He fucked me up. He fucked me up.'"

"Last words," said Gi-Gi. "Nobody wants last words like that."

"Like twelve hours later, we're right here for the fish fry and there's the chalk outline still on the floor and we're walking over and around it."

"It would have been disrespectful to step on it."

"We toasted him. We had that moment of silence there," Gi-Gi reminded him.

"Every time somebody stepped over that outline, we laughed," said Eddie. "What was wrong with us?"

"We were young. When you're young everything is kinda funny."

"Not the way I remember being young."

"Whose bright idea was it to let Shaky the cop draw that outline? Shaky wasn't much of an artist."

"Last time he had chalk in his hand was fifth grade. As far as he got."

Even Eddie chuckled a little.

"It looked like the Roadrunner fell through the floor!" said Gi-Gi, and they laughed out loud.

They drank to Chewie's memory.

"I never ate fish again," said Eddie.

"Any excuse for a Catholic."

67

Birds of a Feather

LIKE GRANDMOTHERS EVERYWHERE, Docia said, "Good job, Noah. That was lovely." She elbowed Stewart to spread a little praise upon his grandson, but Stewart was a poet devoted to the truth.

When she informed him the day before that they were going to "Grandparents Appreciation Day" he said, "Didn't we just do that?" She said, "Yes, a year ago."

Once there, he enjoyed the show as each class took the stage and either sang or danced or read original poetry. Some of them could not get through it without the giggles. Noah's second grade class read their own three-line poems, about birds, which had been a unit of study.

"Mocking birds are cool/They sing so nice/They are awesome."

"I love hawks/They are cool/They fly high."

"Owls are wise/They are awesome/They go hoot."

When it was Noah's turn, the old poet held his breath.

Noah read, "Blue Jays are awesome/They are so cool/I wish I could fly."

"Didn't Noah write a lovely poem?" his wife prodded again.

"Well, kid, you put yourself into the picture, and that was good. Even though you're a higher life form, you envy the simple blue jay. But the rest was derivative."

Noah had no idea what "derivative" meant and didn't care to find out. He understood his old grandpa was a poet, but he never thought about how that might play into anything that he would care about.

"Good *night*," said Docia. "Derivative of what?"

"Of the seven kids ahead of him."

She rolled her eyes and reminded him that the boy was in second grade. She walked over to say something nice to Noah's teacher.

"Why did you pick the blue jay?" Stewart asked.

"The hawk and the eagle and the raven were all taken."

"And why did you say the blue jay was cool and awesome? Everybody else already said that about their own birds."

"Mr. Patterson told us to 'press our feelings about the birds. We all thought they were all cool and awesome."

"If we look into it," the old man said to the boy, "we might find much more to say about the blue jay."

"What?" asked the second grader.

The poet took the boy's hand and they walked toward his teacher and his grandmother.

"I'll get back to you," he said.

Stewart worked on it late into the night, scribbling down some lines, rewriting, deleting. He fell asleep at his desk, which was not unusual for him, and when he awoke, he conceded that little Noah and his classmates got it right.

68

Recapitulation

CARLOS AMUSED HIMSELF by showing up wherever Udo lectured on the subject of Carlos Castaneda. During the Q & A, Carlos would rise to his feet and declare that the professor's subject was no more than a common fraud conning gullible readers hungry for alternatives. A comment like that was sure to stir up the crowd of Castaneda devotees and annoy the speaker, who was, after all, an expert and sick of this heckler.

After one of these lectures at UCLA, Carlos approached Udo and properly introduced himself. Udo was stunned, disbelieving at first, then crying out, "I wondered about you! Following me all around! I saw you in Torrance and I saw you in Ojai and I saw you in San Pedro."

"Impossible," Carlos said, grinning.

"So, by now you must know that I am a genius."

"I can see that," said Carlos.

"Tell me, what would Don Juan say if he knew that all I have is fifty cents a day for food and a dollar a day for cigarettes?"

Carlos imagined Don Juan laughing over a situation like that.

"I'm sure he would think it unfair, a genius like you."

Udo told him that he had sent his impressive Vita to every college and university in the country. Only Muhlenberg College, a small liberal arts college in Allentown, Pennsylvania, replied. They offered to send him an economy ticket on a cut-rate airline and provide him with a modest honorarium to deliver a lecture on Carlos Castaneda to students and faculty.

"I arrived a day early in order to look over the venue, and of course I was able to eat free at the student union."

The programmer in charge told Udo of a rumor that a representative from Harvard was coming to hear his lecture, a scouting trip because Harvard intended to enlarge their anthropology department. Muhlenberg, unfortunately, had no anthropology department.

"It was what I dreamed of my entire academic life, to teach at Harvard. The pinnacle of all my aspirations."

That night, alone in a dormitory room, Udo labored over his notes, polishing and rechecking his details. At five PM the following day, with butterflies in his bowels, he appeared behind the lectern in the time honored pattern of such things and began to present the lecture of his life.

Ten minutes into it, he noticed a man come into the auditorium and stand for a moment in the back, contemptuously looking over the audience. Udo recognized that look. He knew a Harvard man when he saw one. He had employed that look often enough himself. The late-comer was casually, if not carelessly, dressed and looked generally annoyed. He walked to the front row as though he owned the place and slouched down on a seat, prepared to be bored.

"To hell with these bumpkins from Allentown, I thought. I decided on the spot to recapitulate for the benefit of Harvard, so that he would fully appreciate not only the substance but also the structure of my lecture."

Nothing is more boring than having to sit through a recapitulation of what you've already heard, but Udo had in his mind reduced the audience to one. Let them think whatever they want. His academic future was at stake. He concluded his lecture, which he considered a triumph and a half, but he received only a spattering of weak applause. More than half the audience left before the Q & A, including Harvard, and those who remained asked the usual questions.

"I was undone, humiliated and, frankly, insulted. I had little appetite, but I managed to get down a free dinner of pierogi and a diet Coke at the student union. As I was leaving for the airport with my student escort I saw the man from Harvard halfway down the stairs. Would you like to know what he was doing?"

"Going over his notes?"

"No, he was mopping the floor."

69

Problem Child

HARRY AND THIS other man, younger than Harry and borderline obese in a ball cap, were the only ones left in the waiting room. Together they had watched an hour of brisk traffic, women going in and coming out again, collecting their waiting husbands and whispering on their way out of the Desert Breast Center.

He enjoyed striking up conversations with strangers but was at a loss for something to say in this situation. "Isn't this a bitch?" was all he could say, and he wasn't sure he should have said that.

The other man agreed, though.

"My wife's been in there most of the morning," Harry said.

"I brought my girlfriend down from Big Bear."

"You live up there?"

"Yeah, I'm pretty much retired."

"Me too."

"Took us two hours to get here."

"That's not bad."

"I didn't think it would be so hot, this early in June."

"Oh, it can get really hot in June. June can be the hottest month."

Intense heat in the desert is always worth some discussion,

compare and contrast, high and low.

"Was sixty degrees this morning when we left. Now I'm down to my T-shirt."

"Everyone wears shorts and tank tops. Not me. I look ugly in them."

"Me too."

"And you get these pre-cancers on your legs."

The other man kept to the subjects of the heat and the drive and the desert and the mountains. Harry had never been to the mountains because he was told the drive was dangerous.

"They sure are busy here."

"Yeah. Makes you wonder what's going on," said Harry. He didn't want to be grim about it. "I mean, generally speaking."

"Only goes to show you."

"Yeah." And then another woman was led into the inner sanctum. "With Louise, my wife, it's the right one. She calls it her Problem Child." Harry thought that mildly funny.

"My girlfriend's got something going on with both of 'em."

Harry repeated what he said before: "It's a bitch."

He was about to ask the man about baseball—he wore a Dodgers cap—when the girlfriend came back into the waiting area. The poor woman was emaciated, but Harry had the feeling she had always looked that way. She wore a tank top. She was flat-chested. Her breasts were still there but you could hardly notice them. Harry felt bad that he even noticed.

The boyfriend got to his feet with a low groan. Harry hoped the news would be good for them.

The girlfriend smiled wanly and said, "Well, shoot, I have to come back again."

"Again? Why?"

"Their machine broke down."

She seemed crestfallen.

"Now, that's all right," said her boyfriend. "If you have to come back, you have to come back."

"I'm sorry."

"It's okay, don't give it another thought."

"It's okay?"

"Sure. You'll find somebody to bring you back down here."

She laughed first, and then Harry could as well. The boyfriend smiled.

They went back to Big Bear, where it was cool. Harry waited alone, but soon other couples arrived, parting at the inner door as each woman was summoned.

70

Love Letters

AT AGE ELEVEN, Guy attended his first wedding ever, his mother's. Dapper in his little tuxedo, he escorted her down the aisle and gave her away. Frank, sitting among the guests, had to dab his eyes.

During the reception, Guy mingled and made sure the smaller kids were having fun. Frank was struck by his new maturity. He expected that his son would be elected president of his fifth-grade class on the following Wednesday. Between practice sessions kicking a football, he had helped him construct the posters for his campaign: "Guy is the Guy"

Frank avoided dancing, and he was not going to be made to dance at the wedding of his ex-wife, though he hardly thought of her that way.

He thought of her as the mother of his only child.

Wonder of wonders, little Guy had no reluctance getting out on the dance floor, and he had some moves for a fifth grader. Frank sat alone at a table and drank it in.

A little girl of six or seven years tugged at his sleeve. He didn't recognize her and did not know to whom she belonged. For a moment he thought she was going to make him dance with her.

"Do you have a pencil?" she asked.

"I have a pencil and a pen," he said, relieved that he would not have to dance with a little girl.

"The pencil."

"Okay."

He took the pencil out of his inside pocket and gave it to her.

"Do you have any paper?" she asked. He had paper as well, a mini-sketchbook. He tore a page out of it and gave it to the little girl.

"Are you going to draw me a picture?" he asked her.

"No. Why would I draw you a picture?"

"I was hoping."

"I'm going to write a letter."

"Really? Who to?"

"To Guy. You're his father, aren't you?"

"I am."

"I need a little help."

"Okay. What do you want to say to Guy?"

"I love you."

"You do?"

"Yes!"

Frank took a swallow of white wine and fought back tears for the second time in one afternoon.

"Okay. You could start it with, Dear Guy."

He spelled "Dear" for her. She already knew how to spell Guy and wrote it in block letters.

"What should I say?"

"Whatever feels right is what you should write down."

With great concentration, she printed out: "I love you." She slid the note across the table.

"Don't you want to sign it with your name?"

"No!" she said, then dashed away, leaving it to him to deliver her sentiments.

When Guy returned to the table for a breather after all his

dancing, Frank handed him the slip of sketch paper. Guy read it and said, "I love you too, Pop."

71

Portrait of a Lady

IT WAS A time in which a person of means with a position in French society might hire a private detective to get the goods on a cheating spouse, a time unlike the present except perhaps in that regard.

Madeleine, a dark beauty of culture and sensitivity with many admirers, foremost among them her own husband, Marcel, undertook a discreet inquiry into her husband's activities. The report was scandalous. Marcel was seeing prostitutes.

His pattern was so shamelessly predictable that the detective was able to secure for her a key to a room on the third floor of a two-star hotel on rue Jacob, where Marcel was expected at sixteen-hundred hours by a hardened girl of nineteen.

Madeleine arrived at quarter before the hour and was taken aback to find the whore already there, though not as surprised as the girl herself, who lay upon the bed in no more than a chemise.

When Madeleine identified herself, the girl was neither humiliated nor frightened. She merely found it odd that the wife would appear.

"What is your name?" Madeleine demanded.

"Zizue."

"It is not."

"No, but that is how I am known."

"And how is my husband known?"

"Marcel? I hardly know him at all. Only enough to know what he likes."

"I believe I know that as well." The girl shrugged. "Have you already been paid?"

"No, Madam, because I have not yet performed my services."

"Your price, please."

The girl told Madeleine her rates. She thought it was not extravagant. She took the money from her purse and added a small tip.

"Now, take the money and leave before I stab you in the eye with my hat pin."

Having made the threat, Madeleine thought she might employ the hat pin on her husband when he arrived for his assignation. Instead, she removed the pin, took off her hat, and shook her hair loose. She then removed the rest of her clothes and lay down on the bed, uncovered. Let it be said that after two sons, fifteen and twelve, Madeleine's body was still exquisite. She was only thirty-three, after all. Marcel was fifty.

When he entered the dim room, all cheery from a lunch with God knows whom, Marcel expected to see Zizou, and in his mind that is who he saw. He was already ripping at his own clothes before he realized who it was on the bed.

He clutched his heart. Madeleine thought it appropriate that he should drop dead.

"My God, you are so beautiful," he said. "So, you got my message, good, good. I thought it would be great fun to meet in this shabby hotel and pretend..."

"Pretend all you want, Marcel. And, please, take a moment to enjoy the view. You may never see it again."

With that she dressed and retreated to their country home,

171

where she sponsored a series of artists with her husband's money.

In time she relented and allowed Marcel to visit, but he never saw her naked again, except for looking longingly at the paintings her artists made of her.

72

Sins of the Father

ERNEST WAS PLEASED to see her name come up on his phone. Although they had kept in touch and still called each other "honey," he had not heard from her in several months.

They lived in different states now, with different climates and cultures. They chatted around the general subject of how-are-you, really.

"Busy as ever," he said. "Not enough time in the day and never a day off."

"Well, honey…" she said, and he could hear the quaver in her voice, a voice he could still pick out of a crowd, "…I'm going to get married. Again."

He was at his desk. He leaned back. Once recovered, he said, "Honestly, I'm surprised you haven't before now."

"Silly goose, how could I? I was still in love with you."

"Likewise, honey. Maybe it changes but it doesn't end."

"No, apparently not. Anyway, it's only a piece of paper. That's what everyone says now."

"A powerful piece of paper. Are you having any misgivings?"

"Sure, who wouldn't?"

"Some changes can't even be imagined until they happen."

"Are we talking about you or me?"

"Both of us, of course."

He asked her about the man she would marry. From the name, he sounded like a good sort.

"You deserve all the happiness I'm sure you will have," he said, "for the rest of your life."

"So, I have your blessing?"

"Of course you do."

"We're not having a big to-do."

"Oh, I wouldn't show up, don't worry."

He wondered if this would be the last intimate conversation they would ever have. He could find no past lover's words of comfort. They ended up giving each other permission to go on with their new lives wherever they may turn, with their shared memories tucked away where they belong.

His housekeeper came into his office. He had to say a quick and formal good-bye to the only woman he had ever loved.

"You're late for the confessional, Father," the housekeeper reminded him. "You've got a line-up."

He donned his vestments and hurried toward the sins of others.

73

Death With Dignity

ANOTHER PATIENT WAS called in as the couple left. One more was still in the waiting room. They needed to sit down before going out into the hot parking lot. They talked in whispers. What the husband remembered was the ninety percent thing, while the wife kept hearing the frustrated doctor say, "If Jonas Salk had priced his polio vaccine like Gilead, we'd all have polio today."

"Ninety percent, though, that's good odds, great odds," he told her.

"At a thousand dollars a day. How is that possible?"

"In three months, you could be cured he said."

"Could be, not would be."

"The odds are in your favor. It's a good bet."

"It's ninety-thousand dollars. After one month, insurance decides, anyway. They'll tell us what the odds are. They'll tell us what kind of bet it is." She paused for a moment. "No, they won't tell us anything. They'll ignore us."

"Figure sixty-thousand, more or less, to us. We can do it," he said. "We have to do it."

"It would clean us out."

"What choice do we have? What else can we do?"

"I can die."

"No, you can't. You have to do the first month. Please. You're going to be one of the lucky ones. We have to believe that. They're not going to let you die."

"Yes, they are."

The husband and wife fell silent and glanced at the man still waiting. He looked at them over the top of his magazine, then dropped his eyes again, having witnessed the worst moment of their lives.

74

The Little Mouse

THE NEW HUMAN Resources manager was an English woman named Olivia, a comely brunette with hair sweeping over her fair forehead from left to right. She replaced Ira, who had lost the knack for directing people in an organizational format. Olivia was single, forty-five, wore no jewelry, and had a special smile few rarely saw that dipped slightly at one end. She kept her distance from the other employees who tried to draw her into their social circle, which earned her the nickname, "Ice Queen."

Smith in sales was infatuated with her and went out of his way to engage her in the kind of banter that had worked for him in the past with other female colleagues. Smith, by the way, was his first name. His last name was Maron. When he insisted Olivia call him Smith rather than Mr. Maron, she called him Mr. Smith.

Olivia was in charge of the company retreat that year, held at the Ojai Valley Inn and Country Club. She went about providing a safe place for employees to be themselves. She organized amusing activities, most of which included an open bar.

At the Saturday cocktail party, she moved from group to group doing her best to be both friendly and professional. The other women did not find her that way.

She was continually offered martinis but sipped iced tea instead. She became aware that she was making people uncomfortable, the exact opposite of how she wanted them to feel, so she relented and had a Sapphire Blue martini, straight up, olive.

Smith urgently waved her over to his group, who were standing in a circle holding drinks. He asked her to settle a conjecture. Loosened up a bit from the martini, she stood next to him and let out her smile. Smith felt her warmth and smelled the lilacs.

"We're talking tats," he said. "We all showed and told, and now we're wondering if you have any tattoos. These guys say no way, but I say you do have one, a small one, kind of hidden out of sight. Am I right or wrong?"

Olivia had an uncanny way of reading social situations, which had served her well in the world of business, and she sensed that no one had been talking about tattoos at all. Smith was winging it for the amusement of his colleagues and his own dreams of intimacy.

"You're not wrong," she said and paused for effect. "In fact, you're spot on."

Olivia had been observed pampering her skin with lotions poolside, sitting in a cabaña out of the sun. Some in the circle were surprised that she would ever let a tattoo artist ink her body or that she would tell them about it.

"I knew it!" said Smith. "What and where? Tell all."

"Well, if you must know, it is a little mouse."

"A mouse! Perfect! Where? Please!"

"On my inner thigh. Rather high on the thigh." She blamed her silly rhyme on the martini, but Olivia was always in control.

More people joined the circle wanting to see the little mouse. Olivia told them that would be inappropriate, since she was wearing "trousers."

The following night, at the wrap-up dinner, she wore a

skirt, short but not too short, revealing bare legs that put Smith in a swirl. After dinner everyone gathered at the bar. The men urged her to join them. She begged off, but Smith would not hear of it. The women, she could see, were not keen on having her. Smith offered her his bar stool.

He again pressed her to reveal her tattoo, the little mouse on her inner thigh, high. Olivia had had a martini before dinner and a glass of Chablis with dinner and now was nursing a refill on the wine. The others were drunk or adjacent and assumed she was, too.

Smith let them in a rowdy chant: "Show us the mouse, show us the mouse!"

"Oh, all right."

She stood and ever so slowly began to lift the hem of her skirt. Some of the women would later complain that the act was provocative, and her legs were perfect. The skirt inched up until the edges of her black panties were revealed.

Smith leaned forward for a closer look. "I can't see it. Where's the little mouse?" he asked.

Olivia looked down at her own exposed legs and said, "Oh, dear. My pussy must have eaten it."

Two of the women spit out their drinks and one of the men started seriously choking. Smith fell forward and was unable to get up without assistance. Brucie from Sales witnessed the whole thing and reported it to his superiors, who found it borderline inappropriate but violated no rule.

75

Landmark

CLEVE CURSED ALOUD whoever was calling so early in the morning. He cursed himself for not putting his phone on airplane mode before falling into bed after tending bar until two and meeting up for drinks until three. Even the two chihuahuas that slept with him, Pete and Repeat, grumbled over the intrusion.

"It's great news!"

His brother was on the other end, so loud and cheery Cleve had to put the phone on speaker and hold it away from his body.

"Goddamn, Jess, I was sleeping."

Jess lived on the east coast. It was not early for him. He was unapologetic.

"You can sleep anytime, bro. This is huge, a moment in history. Did you feel the earth shake? It shakes toward justice, bro, it shakes toward justice."

It took a moment, but Cleve caught up.

"Yeah, I figured it would come today, after yesterday and Obamacare."

"Aren't you thrilled?"

"I'm hardly awake."

"I'm thrilled for you, bro. I know you; you can't let yourself get excited, but c'mon! Time to let your hair down and celebrate."

"I tend bar in Palm Springs. I've been listening to bitching for years about lazy husbands, and there's twice as many husbands down here as wives."

"Don't piss on your own great day, bro. It's historic. You can get married now anywhere in the country."

"I don't want to get married."

"You can get married and adopt *children*."

"I got dogs."

"I don't think that's what Mom had in mind."

"What do you care, anyway? You're straight."

"Are you kidding? I'm a divorce lawyer! This market is going to be huge!"

Jess had other people to call. Cleve tried to get back to sleep. A park had been reserved for a city-wide celebration in anticipation of the decision. He would drop by later on his way to work.

76

The Terminator

RICKY WAS TWENTY-SEVEN and had been in the corporate world for six years, not counting a summer internship. This would be his first letter of termination. He was nervous about it.

> *Dear Mr. Finkle,*
>
> *This letter is our formal notification that your position at Allentown Amalgamated has been rendered insupportable due to lack of leadership, effective immediately.*
>
> *After carefully reviewing your performance, and after consultation with colleagues, we have determined that your lack of humanity or concern for anyone at a lower pay grade has made it impossible for the undersigned to continue in his present post. You have demonstrated an unfortunate lack of empathy or even common decency and have with malice created a hostile environment here at AA. Multiple complaints have been made but due to an atmosphere of fear and loathing none has been formally filed. Therefore, your services will no longer be required.*
>
> *Please forward our last paycheck to General Delivery, Morea, Tahiti, where we have accepted a position as a deckhand on a luxury charter, where it is expected our skill set will be more appreciated than at Allentown Amalgamated. Best wishes for your future endeavors.*
>
> *Ricky LaMott*

77

The Odds

KIDS CAN WALK across the casino floor as long as they are with an adult and on their way up to a room. This particular kid and her mother, though, caught the attention of the pit boss, a man who had worked in casinos most of his adult life. The little girl was around eight and she was leading the mom, who was blind and obese. They were nicely dressed and trudging more than walking. They passed the escalator and continued toward the sports book.

The pit boss told one of the other guys to cover for him. He found the kid and her mother at a video poker game, the mother seated and the kid standing next to her, telling her what she had for cards. The mother told the girl which ones to hold. They had time for only that hand before he was on them, letting them know that children weren't allowed.

"I can play the slots on sound, but with poker…" the mother tried to explain. "Besides, the slots are a sucker's game."

"Well, you can't play anything, ma'am, with your little daughter here. You need an adult to help you."

"Granddaughter. Thank you, sir."

He escorted them to the Virginia Street exit and felt the hot blast of August air on his face. He backed up and waited a moment between the air conditioner and the street. The blare of rock music and the bells and whistles of the slots echoed behind him.

The little girl held the old lady's arm, and when the light changed, they walked across the street. They looked worn, like outcasts. The pit boss was about to go back to work, but something extraordinary caught his eye. Crossing the street toward him was a boy of around twelve leading an old blind emaciated man. These two were also nicely dressed and walking in the same downtrodden way. You could put blues music to it. As the two child guides passed each other in the middle of Virginia Street they gave no sign of mutual acknowledgement, which is what the pit boss was expecting to see. It would be natural.

He stayed where he was, to head off the boy and his grandfather, if that's who the old blind man was, from coming into the casino. Over the years he'd had to eject underaged kids from the floor, but never the young leading the blind, and now two in one day. What were the odds?

The pit boss wanted to ask the boy why he didn't say hello to that little girl leading her blind grandmother, like he was leading his grandfather, but they did not try to come into the casino. The boy seemed to know that a man in a suit standing at the door would stop them. Instead, he steered the old man toward the Silver Legacy.

78

Eggshell, Eggshell, Eggshell

A BLAST OF cold December air blew inside the Majestic Billiards when Shaky the cop opened the front door for Chief Sweeney. One or the other had often come inside, officially or just to shoot a rack of pool, but everyone could see this was different. Chief Sweeney had his hand on his holstered gun. Shaky had a service revolver but was ordered years before never ever to remove it from the holster, which was fine by him because he never encountered a problem he could not solve with a good piece of wood. He had in his hand a billy club, as it was called in those days. The Chief's teenaged son, who on rare occasions acted as backup, was with them but unarmed. All of them appeared unsettled by what they had recently seen, which were the bodies of two men shotgunned in their own home, an image that would stay with them for the rest of their lives.

Eggshell was playing eight-ball with a few of the boys, Eddie and Gi-Gi and that gang. When he looked up from his shot and saw their grim faces, he knew the rest of his life would be contained in a single sentence. He missed the shot. Eggshell was never good at pool. Or anything else.

"Put down the cue, hands on the table," said the Chief.

The boys looked from one to the other since no one was named specifically. Then Eggshell put down his cue and stepped

185

back.

"Lean forward, hands on the table. That's a good lad."

Eggshell assumed the position like an expected inconvenience.

Chief Sweeney frisked him and cuffed him and walked him out the front door and into the back of the squad car. He got in behind him. His son got behind the wheel and Shaky took the passenger seat.

"Eggshell, Eggshell, Eggshell," Chief Sweeney said forlornly.

"Yeah," the murderer agreed.

"Your own father. And your uncle. C'mon."

"They didn't feel nuttin', they were drunk."

"Any particular reason?"

"They was on my ass all day, never let up. Kept callin' me stupid because I didn't know the name of the governor."

"Scranton?"

"Like the city? I didn't know. Don't care."

"What did you do with the shotgun?"

"Threw in in the culvert on my way up here."

"Taking it somewhere, was you?"

"Center and Main."

"What for?"

"You know."

The Chief sighed heavily. "What made you change your mind?"

"Didn't have no gloves."

"Didn't have no gloves," the Chief repeated, trying to figure it out.

"My hands got cold."

They rode in silence for a few minutes, until Shaky said,

"Thanks, Jesus, for a cold December."

"Amen," said the Chief.

79

Beneath It All

FRANK EMIGRATED TO Paris late in life after visiting the city several times, always alone. On one of his earlier trips there, he walked aimlessly on the outer edges of Montparnasse around midnight and ran into five kids barely out of their teens prying up a manhole cover. One of the girls noticed him. Frank smiled and gave a wave to let her know he was okay with whatever they were doing. She beckoned him to join them.

"Ou vas-vous?" he asked.

"Sous tout cela!"

He was not fluent. Under everybody?

"We can speak English," she said.

"I can speak French; I just can't understand it." They laughed. "So where are you going?"

"Beneath it all! Come with us if you like."

It was an invitation he could not resist.

He followed her down a metal ladder, descending for longer than he had expected into the darkness. One of the boys closed the lid and came down last. They all had flashlights. It was cold. The silence as they moved was exquisite.

Frank hoped they knew where they were going. The narrow tunnel intersected with others. At each intersection, the leader put his light on a street name carved into the stone: "rue

Noir," "bd. de Balzac," and others. They passed stacks of categorized human bones, from ground to ceiling. Skulls here, arms there, legs somewhere else.

"Don't be afraid," said the girl. "We are expert cataphiles."

"I'm not afraid. What's a cataphile?"

She laughed and then they heard a distant piano playing what sounded to Frank like ragtime. They moved toward the sound and came to a spot where the tunnel split into three directions. An old man sat on a rickety chair, a lantern on the ground next to him. In exchange for five francs, he gave the leader directions Frank could not understand. The cataphiles picked up the pace and soon found a narrow path through stacks of bones to a crevice three feet off the ground. From deep inside the crevice the piano played an upbeat tune. Frank followed the students, crawling into the crevice.

On the other side was a chamber decorated like a 1920s nightclub. It was full of people and illuminated by candles and lanterns. The kids told him it was "Rick's Place." A Maitre d' in a tuxedo showed them to a table. The band was a trio: a battered piano, a bass, and a single snare drum. Frank danced with the young girl, and then with other women who were older. He drank Burgundy, glass after glass. He could not remember when last he danced, or held a woman close, or drank Burgundy. He wondered how they got a piano down there.

Time was not a factor beneath it all. Hours passed without accounting. Eventually the crowd thinned, and he looked around for his guides. They were gone. It must be morning topside.

Frank saw a couple crawl out of the club and tried to go with them, but he was stopped by the Maitre d'. The kids had stuck him with the tab. He didn't mind. He was seeing a Paris he never expected to experience. Settling the bill took a few minutes. He worked himself through the crevice and raced after the couple, following their light. He called after them, "Arrete! S'il vous plait!" The light moved away and Frank was left in total silent darkness. He tried to backtrack feeling his way with his hand against the wall, but he became disoriented.

He sat down with his back against the cold wall and sorted out what might happen: someone could come along and lead him out or he would die in the dark catacombs of Paris. He assumed he wouldn't be the first. His anxiety was momentary. If he was a man lost in life, as people who knew him often believed, then he was where he should be.

He imagined Paris awakening above him, the soft unfurling of another day. He talked to himself about things he might have done and things he should not have done, until he felt foolish. He did what he did, right or wrong, and none of it mattered, beneath it all.

In the distance a flashlight slowly bore down on him, bright as a star. For a moment he thought he was asleep and dreaming. He called out. Soon a gendarme was standing before him, casting a light into his face.

"*Passeport, s'il vous plaît.*"

Frank handed over his passport and thought that if he had to spend a day in a French jail it would be a fair exchange. Instead, the gendarme gave him a stern lecture in French and fined him one hundred francs, to be paid immediately. Frank gave him the cash and ten more francs for his trouble. The gendarme lectured him on the foolishness and danger of his transgressions, and the lecture continued all the way to an exit, where Frank shook the gendarme's hand. More than ever, he loved Paris.

80

Finders Keepers

THE WALLET WAS in plain sight on the ground near the bicycle rack. Watch someone find a wallet and you can expect one of two actions to follow, neither of which this man took. He noticed it before he dismounted and studied it while locking his bike, but never bent down to pick it up. He turned away and walked to the Peninsula French bakery and came out with an almond croissant and a coffee. They have tiny tables in a narrow paseo there. He sat at one of them where he could see if anyone would pick up the lost wallet.

His bicycle was not the kind you would ride a great distance or use regularly for exercise. It was likely his sole means of transportation.

The almond croissant might be a weekly treat to himself. He ate it slowly, pulling it off piece by piece, all the while watching.

The coffee took another ten minutes. Then he had to go back to his bike. No one had discovered the wallet in all that time.

He unlocked his bike but did not pedal away. Again, he stood still and looked down at the wallet as though he were put upon by it. He finally picked it up but did not open it right away. He tapped it against a forefinger, like you might with a pack of cigarettes. When he did open it, he discovered that it was empty of anything that might be carried in a wallet. He smiled. You could call it relief.

He rode his bike past a trash barrel and tossed into it what turned out to be not his problem.

81

"Stars—They're Just Like Us!"

EDDIE, JOEY, AND Gi-Gi had recently taken to drinking fancy cocktails without explanation or apology. It was a noticeable departure from their drinking history and indeed their geographical culture where men like them drank shots and beers.

One day, out of the blue, Eddie asked Kathy if she could make a martini. She was insulted by the question. "Then make one for me, dammit." Eddie said. Joey and Gi-Gi were on either side of him that night and did not know what to make of this. They wondered if it wasn't because of all the reading Eddie was doing lately, stacks of three-month old magazines while waiting in doctors' offices. In any case, Eddie offered a taste to his two friends, who promptly ordered martinis for themselves. The cocktail gave them a pleasant icy numbness on the lips.

Martinis, however, were expensive, the shaking and the olive and all that. Eddie told Kathy she ought to initiate a Happy Hour. All the bars had happy hours now, lasting longer than an hour even. She invited him to go to one of those bars. After further discussion, she relented and said she would mix them martinis or whatever the hell fancy cocktail they wanted at half price, four o'clock to five.

"Don't tell anybody else," she said. "Instead of a martini,

we'll call it a gin up." Which, except for a breath of vermouth and a questionable olive, it was.

In time they moved on to Manhattans. The second time they ordered Manhattans, Eddie raised his voice at Kathy. "Stop! You don't shake it, you have to stir it, and guess what? Those martinis should have been stirred, too!"

The boys believed his new expertise had come from the magazines he was reading in doctors' offices.

"The fuck..." said Kathy, who seldom used language like that.

This particular afternoon, Joey and Gi-Gi were one cocktail up on Eddie by the time he joined them after his appointment. He looked pale and clutched a sheath of pages torn from a magazine. (Which confirmed their theory.)

Eddie peeled off a page, held it at arm's length and read aloud, in a theatrical voice, "Stars—They're Just Like Us!"

"Okay," said Gi-Gi.

"They grab food to go!" Eddie pointed to the picture of a kid in ugly shorts carrying take-out. Scott Eastwood, he was. "They fumble in their bags!" Someone named Olivia Palermo. "They browse menus!" That would be Ed Sheeran. "They slurp soup!" Gavin Rossdale. "They pay for parking!" Hillary Duff at a parking meter.

Kathy put out plastic cups of kibbles and bits, part of the new unadvertised Happy Hour. Eddie spread the pages on the bar and said, "Would you take out the walnuts, sweetheart, they make my cheeks hurt." She stared him down in stony silence. "I'll have an Old-Fashioned!" he announced. Kathy said, "I don't think those stars are anything like you."

"Us," said Eddie. "They're just like us, it says."

"I'm gonna say they're right," said Gi-Gi. "I never heard of any of these stars and they never heard of any of us."

82

Tradition

WHEN YOU DO not know someone's name or can't remember it you call him guy or maybe buddy. If you're a Brit, an Aussie, or a Kiwi, you call him mate.

When Guy became old enough to observe that social convention, he experienced a hurtful sense of anonymity and came to question and later resent his given name. It wasn't related to anything with which he could identify. It had no tradition.

His friends Noah and Gabriel had names right out of the Old Testament, said to be the best part of the Bible.

Children are adaptable but little things bother them, not to suggest that one's name is a little thing. It is something you are given and most of us learn to accept it. Guy, however, filed a complaint. He argued the case to his father that whenever he heard someone call out, "Hey, guy," he would turn around to see who was calling him, and then he would feel foolish. His father tried to assure him that Guy was an elegant name, the name of a famous French writer. He pronounced it for him the way they do in France.

"It sounds Chinese!" cried his son.

The issue would not go away. The boy argued that he would have been happier with his father's name, Frank, though he would not have liked being called Junior. He would have been okay with his grandfather's name, even, which was John. Guy argued that he should have been given the name of an ancestor. Most kids are unhappy at some point in their young lives over their names, but Guy became a pest on the issue.

At the end of his patience, Frank sat him down and told him that if his given name was ruining his life, he could choose a new name. (Guy didn't know you could do that.) And since he thought he should have been given an ancestral name, he would have to choose from the page Frank had obtained from Ellis Island with the list of their forefathers who had immigrated from Hungary to America.

Frank pointed out that his own grandfather had also changed his name shortly after arriving. His real name? Jaws. Guy did not want to be named Jaws. (The popular movie was all but unknown to Guy's generation. Frank himself would have loved being named Jaws.)

"Look here. There's Gusztay or Gyorgy or Jozsef or Karoly or Mileva. Take your pick."

Guy felt boxed in. This was not going as he thought it would.

"I can't even *say* those names, and I can't spell them either."

"Well, we've got four more names on the list, easy ones," Frank told him. "Say them out loud, see how they sound."

"Pal, Pal, Pal, and Mate?" read Guy, mystified.

"So, in a way," said Frank, "your name follows a tradition."

"Okay, I'll take Pal," Guy said.

"How does that solve your problem? You're going to hear someone call, 'Hey, pal,' and you'll turn around thinking it's you."

"Yeah, I can see that happening."

"Would you like to sleep on it, decide in the morning?"

"Okay."

Overnight, Guy made peace with the name he had been given and never again brought up the subject.

Darryl Ponicsán

83

What to Tell Alice

"HOW'S ALICE?"

It was always his second question and one that needed a sincere answer.

"Healthy and happy," said the young mother. "Doing well in pre-school."

Clive was one of her few friends and the last of her male friends. They got together for lunch now and then and talked about their jobs, then Alice again, and how she was. Really.

"She's fine, honestly. She's a jewel, the joy of my life."

"You ought to get yourself a pre-dated husband," he said.

"You?" she asked, smiling.

"I love you too much."

"I was kidding."

"Okay. You're going to have to lie, you know, and you're not that good at that."

"Oh, I'm improving."

"And the lie would have to hold forever. Few lies manage. What are you going to say when she finds out, because she will?"

"She doesn't have to."

"But she will."

"Then I'll ask forgiveness and hope she'll understand. I think she will."

"Well, you did go through with it, you made the hard choice. She should love you for that at least. Only a lie is worse than the thing, most times."

"Not this time. It will make her life easier. I'll tell her bits of things that might be true."

"Like what?"

"These days I tell her that her father would have loved her as much as I do."

"Really?"

"That's not necessarily a lie."

"No, it's a false assumption."

"It could be true, could have been."

"It's grotesque. God, next you'll wind up apologizing for it. I'm sorry. That sounded mean."

"Maybe we can talk about something else now."

"She'll want to know his name and what he looked like and why you don't have any pictures and how did he make a living."

"I'll make up something. All I really know about him is that one thing."

"That's my point. It would be the defining thing in her life."

"We'll have that in common."

"But she'll be the result, not the victim."

"What difference does it make?" The sweet potato fries had gone cold. She dropped the unbitten part back on her plate. "Clive? Be a better friend and never bring it up again."

84

Triple Aces

VIRGINIA HAD HAD enough birthday parties. She stopped enjoying them after she turned 100. Staff set them up, and the local press and TV people from the city attended them. This one was her 111th, or as her oldest great-great-grandson dubbed it, Triple Aces. The last of her living children, Melanie, attended the party in a wheelchair pushed by her own caretaker. She was 88 and in worse health than her mother.

The cake was white from the top and throughout. They all sang Happy Birthday, dear Virginia. She knew the question would come. She tried to remember what she had said the year before. They aimed a camera at her. A smiling young Mexican girl put a microphone in front of her face and asked, "To what do you attribute your longevity, Virginia?"

She had lived through two depressions, two pandemics, and two world wars. She saw the invention of the radio, which killed board games, and television, which killed radio, and the internet, which killed most everything. She buried two husbands, all but one of her children, a fair number of her grandchildren—she'd forgotten how many she had—and all of her true friends, every last one of them.

"Just my dumb luck," she told the reporter, and for some reason everyone laughed and applauded.

85

Up in Smoke

THE CHILDREN WERE off on their own and she would be too if she had anywhere to be off to. She was up to *here* with her husband's drinking but resigned to waiting him out.

To anticipate the personality that might surface when he was fully drunk was like shaking dice out of a leather cup onto the bar. You never knew and you could not guess. Odds were five to two he would be argumentative; six to one he'd be sweet and sloppy; even odds on Godzilla emerging.

On the night in question, he ranted on that Mexicans were taking over the country and it was high time to take it back if America was ever going to be great again.

"I would like to remind you that we have a Mexican daughter-in-law that even you adore," she said, which should have been enough, but she followed up by reminding him that burritos had become his staff of life.

It is difficult for devout Christians to imagine that such ideas could escalate to the screaming level, but scream they did, back and forth, until he stormed out to the side yard yelling, "White lives matter!" and something about the deep state.

"Some white lives!" she yelled after him. "And look at the state you're in!"

He had a disabled '62 Chevy Malibu in the yard, and he

escaped to it whenever her stupidity threatened to gain the upper hand. The Chevy's trunk was always agape, with a mover's blanket spread on the floor, inviting him to crawl into the cocoon safety of the space for a nap after a contentious encounter.

This time, however, feeling a chill as he fell asleep, he reached up and pulled the trunk lid shut, as though he were in bed covering himself with a quilt.

In the morning, he woke up disoriented, but soon pieced together where he was and how he got there. He could not open the trunk from the inside. He banged at it and yelled between expletives for his wife to find the key and set him free. She was fast asleep with the chihuahua under her arm and heard none of it, she later testified. His anger having returned in a wracking hangover, he tore at the back seat, pulling away wads of stuffing. It was slow going and dark as the inside of your pocket. Like most alcoholics he was a smoker, unfiltered Camels, and always carried a lighter. He ignited it to see his progress. The stuffing caught fire, as anyone with a dry brain would have foreseen. He crushed the small flame easily enough with his sleeved elbow, but the trunk filled with smoke.

Cause of death: smoke inhalation.

It would have been mid-way down on her list of expectations, somewhere between stroke and gun shot.

86

Sometimes You Get the Abalone: Two Cautionary Tales

1

ABALONES DON'T TRAVEL well. They find something they can attach to and stay put, safe from most predators because of how difficult it is to remove them. That is, except by a diver with a pry bar.

The free-diver was down only twenty feet when he saw the abalone in a crevice and went for it. He reached in with his bar, but it proved harder to pry the shellfish off than he expected. He would have to surface, take in some air, and try again. He kicked up, but the pry bar was jammed in the crevice.

A more experienced diver would have known that you tether nothing to your body that can hold you underwater. The pry bar was looped tight around his wrist and so he drowned.

The abalone took no notice.

2

THE SCUBA DIVER was at eighty feet, separated from his dive buddy, which happens almost all the time.

His game bag already held a limit of abalones, but he thought he'd take one extra in case anybody on the boat was short at the end of the day. He pried the abalone off the rock easily enough and put it into his bag.

At that moment he found it hard to suck any more air out of his tank.

He dropped the game bag, the pry bar, and his weight belt as he was trained to do. He did not panic. He expected to make a controlled ascent to the surface.

Rescue and recovery divers discovered him upright, as though standing on the ocean floor, swaying with the current. His weight belt hung over the crotch strap of his floatation vest.

87

Curbside Recycling

STEWART'S WIFE HAD laryngitis and didn't want to go that week, so he went alone to the farmers' market in the park. He walked there, carrying his collapsable chair, his shoulder bag, and a bottle of chardonnay in an ice bag. His cargo wasn't all that heavy, but it was a long walk and halfway there he was sorry he didn't ask for a ride. At least his return trip would be lighter by losing the weight of the wine, the bottle, and the ice.

He set up under the big cork tree, near the music, and looked around for anyone he might know. He bought some oysters and chips from a stand and drank his wine while he read the evening paper. (He would lose the weight of that, too.) A woman who painted in watercolors, lilies mostly, stopped to say hello. One of the city councilmen came by and told him he was working on establishing a Poet Laureate position for the city and planned to recommend Stewart for that honor. Stewart told him he would rather the council ban leaf blowers so that he could work at home in peace and quiet.

He finished the wine, emptied the remaining ice onto the grass, tossed the bottle and the newspaper into the blue barrel, and collapsed his chair. The load was not as heavy, but his gait was not as steady. He texted Docia and asked her to pick him up at the northeast corner of the park. She texted back that she was on her way.

Stewart carried his chair to the corner and stood at the crosswalk. He stood until he was tired. "Slowest woman in the northern hemisphere," he muttered. He set up his chair on the curb and sat down to wait.

In his youth, he enjoyed sitting somewhere and watching the cars go by. Everyone did in those days. You would sit in groups and talk and watch the cars and say something to the people passing by on foot. He had forgotten how pleasant time spent like that was and now did not mind that it was taking her so long to fetch him.

A police car passed through the intersection, then parked at an angle. The cop behind the wheel asked him what he was doing. Stewart told him, "Watching whatever goes by."

The remark was a statement of fact without inflection, but it got the cop out of his car. He stood over Stewart and asked him why he was doing that.

"Watching whatever goes by. I used to when I was a boy. We used to call out the cars—Chevy, Ford, Olds—now they all look alike."

"Have you been drinking?"

"Like everyone in the park. Chardonnay."

"Are you drunk?"

"What's the difference? I'm sitting in a chair."

"Where do you live?"

"About a mile from here."

"Well, you're going to have to move on."

"Why's that?"

"You're obstructing the sidewalk."

"Technically, I'm on the curb. You can walk behind me on all the sidewalk you need, or you can walk in front of me, without any danger of...of anything."

"Okay, c'mon, out of here."

The cop looked to be only in his thirties and already

offended about more than just Stewart, who said, "I'm not bothering anybody."

Though a cop of any age believes the badge deserves respect, Stewart set about convincing him that a poet of seventy-seven deserves it more. Docia arrived before he could make his case, which might have prevented his arrest for...whatever.

Darryl Ponicsán

88

#don'tsayhisname

FRANK REMEMBERED THE place as a nice town just off the interstate, friendly people, rained a lot. He stopped there once on a motorcycle trip from Seattle to Oakland.

He remembered calling a local barber from the motel. It was almost five and the barber was closing his shop. Frank explained to him that he needed a shave, badly, and a haircut, just as badly. He had to lose the beard before tomorrow because his ex-wife could not bear to look at facial hair. The barber said he would wait for him.

Afterwards, shorn and shaven, he rode to a Mexican restaurant that was close to the I-5 and his motel, where he could have a couple of Bohemia beers without too great a risk of going off the road later. The food there was authentic and the people welcoming. He kept rubbing his face. It felt undressed now that the beard was gone. He felt as safe there in Roseburg as anywhere else.

Now, so far from Oregon, he read on his iPad that a young man in that nice town killed ten people unknown to him. Nor did the victims know him. Nobody knew him. The carnage occurred on the campus of a community college.

The shooter was one of a heavily studied generation. When asked by researchers to list their important goals, most of them answered, "To be famous." It became known as "The Kardashian Syndrome." A generation, it seemed, that wanted to be noticed, widely and for anything. This particular shooter, reacting to another random slaughter in another nice town, wrote online, "A man who was known by no one is now known by everyone. His face splashed across every screen, his name across the lips of every person on the planet. All in the course of one day."

Frank saw the anger in that, much like anyone else's, under the unfelt lament. Was the shooter proving a point by imitating the monster? Did it matter?

In their grief the people of Roseburg needed to act upon the killer, to punish him, to deprive him of more than his freedom. What of any significance could they do to him? What did he have left? "Don't say his name," they told each other, and everyone in town agreed. His name was never to be written or spoken again by anyone who lived in Roseburg, including the local press.

Frank read about this event and its aftermath on his tiny balcony in Paris. When evening fell, he turned off the device and looked down at rue Delambre. The Harley Frank had ridden into and out of Roseburg was sold long ago. He would never go back to see if the promise held.

"Qu'est-ce que c'est?" his lover asked, crawling out of the window with his bourbon on the rocks in one hand and her red wine in the other.

"America," he said. "Encore."

She nodded. She didn't need to hear more. They clinked their glasses together.

"Today brought us nothing," he said, "but I'm grateful it didn't take anything away."

She spoke English but not well. She raised his arm and put it around her shoulders. He pulled her closer.

89

Busboy

THE SEVENTEEN-YEAR-OLD busboy first caught a glimpse of the handsome young Senator when he delivered room service to his suite, which was full of people in suits.

That night the hotel kitchen was noisy, even at midnight, when the same people breezed through it, happy over the success of the California primary. Juan reached out to shake Robert Kennedy's hand. He heard the shot but didn't recognize it as one. Everyone rushed to bring down the shooter, but the bus boy stayed with the Senator, falling with him, keeping his hand under his bleeding head so that it would not have to lie on the cold concrete. He lowered his ear close to the man's moving lips.

"Is everyone okay?" he asked in a faint voice. Juan said to him, "Yes, everybody's okay." He felt a warm stream of blood running through his fingers.

Juan took his rosary beads out of his pants pocket and laced them into the Senator's hands so that they would not drop away.

Forty-two years passed. Juan made his living paving driveways. He worked hard and tried to live an honorable life. Not a day passed without the memory. In 2010, he bought his first suit of clothes and travelled to Arlington National Cemetery to visit Robert Kennedy's grave.

When he returned, he tried to express to his family the odd emotion that flowed over him, much like the blood through his fingers all those years before.

"I felt American," he told them.

90

The Mystique of the Professional Place Kicker

IT IS BELIEVED with only scant evidence that the head of a professional place kicker can be entered and vandalized. Elite kickers in the NFL, however, have sealed the vault. Though snow falls upon the gridiron, they feel no cold. Though outlandish taunts reach their ears, they might as well be in Greek. Though time-out is called a mini-second before the snap, the elite place kicker turns away, takes a stroll, and comes back to where he was before he was rudely interrupted with confidence and concentration intact.

The place kicker has the innate ability to be alone without feeling lonely. He never has to touch a football with either hand during competition, except perhaps to fondle it before sending it away like a message in a bottle. He himself is rarely ever touched by another player and is considered by the rules to be a delicate creature. To bump into him is a personal foul and costly to the offender's team.

Place kickers score more points and win more games than players in other positions, including the quarterback, though their playing minutes are measured in single digits. Likewise, they lose more games and receive in equal measure expressions of both love and hatred. No matter, they live for those 1.3 seconds between the placement of the ball and the contact of the toe, and when no other path to victory or survival is likely for a team in arrears, the impossible is asked of them.

During what became known as the "Raiders Renaissance," post-Janikowski, with three seconds on the clock and down a single point against the disgraced and despised Patriots, and with no other viable options, Guy was sent in to kick a seventy-one-yard field goal, something no one on earth had ever done before. This is the play beyond the Hail Mary, loosely rooted in the belief that miracles do happen. If he made it, the Raiders would go into the play-offs. If he missed it…well, it was expected that he would miss it. The coach was hoping for a roughing-the-kicker foul and a replay closer to the goal posts. Dream on.

The record for the NFL at that time was sixty-four yards. Oddly, both college and high school kickers have booted sixty-nine-yard field goals. Guy himself had kicked a few sixty yard three-pointers, but he did not practice much beyond that range because there seemed no point to it beyond horsing around.

The Raiders called time to set up the kick, then just before the snap New England called time, to ice the kicker.

Guy would not be iced. His teammates huddled on the side lines. No one had anything to say. Guy stood on the field alone. He appeared unaware of where he was.

Then he took a knee and bent forward.

The crowd fell silent except for a murmur of boo's. It was the wrong time to make a political statement.

His father, Frank, was in the stands, on his feet. The knuckles of one hand had been clamped between his teeth. Now he wondered if this was the culmination of all their hard work: taking a knee. Guy had kicked thousands of footballs out from under Frank's forefinger, starting when he was eight, first kicked nowhere but up, but later cleanly between the goal posts. Frank had it all mapped out. "The kicker never gets hurt," he told Guy.

"You can get a scholarship to Stanford."

That came to pass. Guy set school records and earned a BA degree in Environmental Systems Engineering. Now he was making five-point-five million dollars a year kicking a football, which eventually proved to be an embarrassment to him. No one is worth that for doing that. He had a friend, a teacher at a community college, who made about fifty thousand a year for work far more important than Guy's, though his friend disagreed. Women were drawn to him, but he could not trust their reasons.

Guy, however, had no intention of making a political statement. He knelt in order to remove his shoe and sock. He stood and tossed them to the side. Now the crowd cheered, relieved that he was not going through a career-ending political protest. The fans were confused, frightened and unsteady atop a bubbling excitement. A perplexed manager ran out and carried the shoe and sock off the field. Guy's teammates looked at him in horror. Some kickers made a practice out of bare-footing, but Guy was not one of them. Did he have a secret? Had he been holding something back for just this moment?

In the stands, Frank had grave misgivings. To his knowledge his son had never kicked with a bare foot. Why choose a frigid December in New England in front of a hostile crowd, with everything on the line, including a world record, to start now?

The two teams trotted back to the line of scrimmage.

Guy paced his measured three steps backwards and two to the left. He nodded to the holder.

The snap was perfect, the hold flawless.

Guy executed the three-step attack that would forever be part of his kinetic memory and he kicked with everything he had, suspending himself in the follow-through, his body in the air for an inordinate time, though not nearly as long as the ball. His father might have been the only one whose eyes were not following the arcing ball. He was looking at Guy, who landed on his back in pain. Everyone else watched the ball, sailing end over end, seemingly gathering momentum rather than losing it.

When the football cleared the uprights with space enough for a hummingbird's wing, the spectators collectively lost their minds. Even the New England fans cheered Guy, while at the same time wishing him dead. His teammates rushed to him and tossed him into the air. But first they had to pick him up. His foot was broken. Carried on the outstretched hands of his teammates, he held his career-ending injury aloft and laughed through the pain.

91

The Pirate

OWEN'S WIFE JUNE did not drink, nor care for bars, but she drove him to the places he liked and sat with him on wobbly bar stools to keep him from drinking alone, though drinking alone never seemed to bother him.

At one of those bars, he tried to talk to her about what life might be like for them in the near future, as a couple, but June was distracted by the array of liquor bottles against a mirrored wall. They stood in tiers, like members of a secular choir.

"Rip Van Winkle," she said. "Have you ever had that one?"

"No," said Owen, though he might have. At the moment, he was having a Manhattan, at the bottom of which lay a black cherry speared by a plastic pick.

"It's a lovely label. You ought to try it."

"Memo to myself."

"Such beautiful labels, don't you think? A lot of creativity went into designing them. You can see that. They pull in the eye in a strange way."

"Really?"

"How is it all arranged? Is there a plan? If a bottle is removed, do they know which one takes its place?"

"Do you care, or are you changing the subject?"

"I'm curious. The choices seem...well, not endless, but..."

"The best stuff is on the top, the cheaper stuff on the bottom. It's pretty simple."

"Is that where the expression, 'Top shelf' came from?"

"I wouldn't be surprised."

"But nothing stays on the top shelf forever."

"Some do, the classics. The cheapest booze is in the well."

"What well?"

"The tank below the bar. You can't see it from here."

"I didn't know about the well."

Owen knew she would go on about liquor bottles and their labels and how they were arranged, eventually drawing other people into the conversation, people who would then become her friends.

"Look at that one. Pyrat. Is that how you say it? Or is it Pirate?"

"I don't know. It's rum."

"I love that bottle. It's so inviting."

"You want to try it? With Coke?"

"I'm driving."

"It's top shelf."

"Maybe someday," she said. Owen thought it unlikely. "Where is it made?"

"I have no idea."

She called the bartender over, as Owen expected she might.

"That rum there," she said, "the Pyrat, is it good?"

"Ah, you see, I'm not a bartender," he said.

"She's not a drinker," said Owen.

"I'm a server, but I'm filling in for the regular bartender. He's a little late. He'll be here, though, any minute now. Please don't order a mojito."

"I'm curious where that rum is made?" she asked the young man who was not a bartender but was behind the bar mixing drinks anyway. Not the difficult ones.

"Let it go," said Owen. "He told you he's not a bartender."

"Aren't you curious?"

"Not about that bottle of rum."

The server took down the bottle and put it on the bar.

"Let's find this out together," he said.

She smiled at Owen. See? She was happy now. She followed the young substitute's fingertip along the fine print on the back of the bottle.

"Anguilla!" she cried out.

She regarded it as a small wonder. Anguilla. None of them knew exactly where Anguilla was or knew anyone who had ever gone there. She wanted to go to Anguilla as soon as possible. Tomorrow maybe.

Owen, the only serious drinker of the three, would have guessed the rum came from Barbados, gun to the head.

92

Dream Big

ANTONIO WAS HIMSELF a product of public art. As a middle-schooler in his own barrio, he would analyze street graffiti and socially conscious murals for extra credit, and the credit accrued to his account. He became an artist.

He was working on a four-thousand square foot mural under the overpass on the 580 freeway at 35th Street, Oakland, volunteering in a grassroots anti-violence campaign. He believed in the power of art to change the human heart. He believed that art could inspire young people to dream big. That would be the title of his mural: "Dream Big."

A group of teenagers had signed up to join him the next day to help him finish it. They all lived in better places. He wondered if it might be confusing for them. What's so big about kids walking down a peaceful tree lined street of little homes? That's all that Antonio's mural portrayed, on the surface.

Looking at art was better than not seeing it at all, but Antonio hoped his work would do more.

A young man approached the site as Antonio was working from the scaffold. He gave the mural no more than a glance before he started rifling through Antonio's box of supplies, his jacket, his lunch.

"Can I help you?" Antonio asked him for his perch.

"Fuck you, *pendejo*."

"C'mon, don't be a dick."

The young man drew a gun and held it horizontally, like in the movies. He shot the artist and ran away.

Antonio fell, and as he lay dying, he looked up at his painting and felt himself pulled into it.

93

The Most Beautiful Woman in America

THE ACTRESS, A former model, had been named "The Most Beautiful Woman in America" by one of those magazines that do that.

The screenwriter from Reno was staying at the Hollywood Roosevelt during the two-weeks of rehearsals. The actress, who lived in New York, had a rented bungalow in Santa Monica for the duration. It was a low-budget independent film.

Three days into a two-week rehearsal, he had lunch at the Dome with the two leads and the director. The director was in the habit of saying something disparaging about anyone who had just left the conversation. He would fawn over someone until the person walked away and then he might say, "What a sick shit he is." In the case of the leading man, who left the lunch early, this was probably true. The actress stayed at the table longer, maybe to delay whatever he might say about her.

They tried to talk about something other than the script but found the script was the only thing they had in common. The director gushed about the poetry in it, which made the screenwriter reluctant to leave the table. The actress said the script was "manna from heaven," and she ran a few of her favorite lines. When she finally left to prepare for their afternoon session, the director said, "Psycho bitch. She's going to destroy us. She doesn't have the chops for a script like this. Listen, every chance you get, put her in her underwear."

The screenwriter ignored that note. "I'm not worried," he said. "She's a little awkward because she's feeling her way into the character. Her character loves this guy. That's a stretch for her. She's the most beautiful woman in America and he's ugly as an open wound. Don't worry, she'll come through."

The director told him she wasn't that smart. The leading man, the sick shit, was in a panic she would ruin his career. The director gave a spot-on imitation: "It's gonna be my face up there. I'll be totally exposed. Do something!" Then he pretended to cry.

It was not too late to fire her and find somebody else, the director mused. The character had to be beautiful, in contrast to her over-achieving husband, but she did not have to be the most beautiful woman in America.

The screenwriter thought it would be a mistake to replace her.

"Take her out, will you?" the director asked him.

"Out of the script? Are you crazy?"

"No, just take her out. To dinner. She's all alone in LA. Get her to relax. Get her to eat. She needs to gain a few pounds. She looks anorexic."

The screenwriter never imagined a date with the most beautiful woman in America, but when he asked her, she said, yes, she'd like that. He took her to Musso and Frank's, true Hollywood. She needed no coaxing to eat. She polished off a thick pork chop. She was good company, open, not at all full of herself, as one might expect.

"You know what I love to do more than anything?" she said.

"Act?"

"Dance! And sing, but I'm better at dancing. Would you please write a musical for me?"

"I don't know anything about musicals," he said. "My reality doesn't include bursting into song."

He didn't know much about drugs either, which is what their movie was about, and what most movies are about.

She lowered her voice and asked him sincerely, "Are you worried about me?"

"No. The director is."

She looked worried. "I know what I'm doing. Honest."

"I believe you. What are you doing?"

"He's so fragile I have to skate around him," she said, talking about the leading man. "He's afraid I'm going to steal the movie. It has him in a panic. And I *will* steal this movie."

He encouraged her to do so.

After dinner, he took her to see "Postcards" at the Beverly Center. They held hands half-way through the show and at the door to her bungalow she kissed him good-night. A pleasant surprise.

They got along well during the rehearsal time and enjoyed the shoot that followed. The director and the leading man continued to live in anxiety, but most people in Hollywood do.

The movie premiered with little fanfare and quickly tanked. It was said to be too grim, and whoever was saying it was not wrong. Reviews were positive, though, and critics singled out the actress. She won a Golden Globe and was nominated for an Oscar. The leading man was overlooked, as was the screenwriter and the director, who confided to others in the industry that he could never overcome the problems in the script.

Despite that, the director offered the screenwriter another project, but he turned it down and stayed in Reno. He moved into the El Dorado for a few weeks and tried to write a musical that took place in a casino like that.

94

Halle Berry

EDDIE CAME INTO the bar with his right hand held aloft, a fistful of torn magazine pages squeezed in his grip. He appeared both depressed and hopeful, like a man with a major problem and a long-odds solution, which happened to be the case. The boys were sipping Cosmopolitans, having made fancy cocktails their new diversion. Behind the bar, Kathy saw Eddie come in like that and said, "What now?"

"Halle Berry," Eddie said, a deep sadness in his voice.

"Jesus," said Kathy.

"It went bad again. How can this be happening?" He smoothed out one of the pages on the bar with both hands and ordered a daiquiri, or as he called it, a Doc Greenie. He tapped his finger on the face of Halle, who in the picture was smiling like the Mona Lisa, and he said, "This is the gold standard for womanhood. How much better can it get? God didn't short her on anything. Who would strike this woman? Who would cheat on her? She's an angel."

"Calm down."

"Look at her!"

Gi-Gi and Joey agreed she was a beautiful lady. "How is this any business of yours?"

"I feel so helpless."

These men were not shy about ridiculing one another's emotions, but this thing, they could see, might be out of bounds.

"There's still a chance," said Eddie, smoothing out another page.

"Chance 'a what?"

"Strengthening her core. She's got to go inward to go forward."

He showed his friends the illustrated directions for slow breathing exercises. He had tried it himself, he told them, not more than an hour ago, and it calmed him down.

"I'm not sure it did," said Joey.

"It centered me."

"In the middle of what?"

Eddie ignored that and went on: "You sit in a comfortable position and make a hang ten sign with your hand. You hold your thumb over the right nostril to plug it. You inhale through the other one, slow, and hold it for a few seconds. Let go of that nostril and put the pinkie on the other one and exhale. Reverse and repeat."

In no time he had them practicing it.

"Kathy, give it a try."

"I work in the hospitality business," she said. "I'm not going to be putting fingers up my nose."

(Though she did try it at home.)

"Somehow I've got to get this to Halle," said Eddie. "It's a start. It's something, something she can control. You know this is going to happen again, next man, unless she gets a grip on herself."

"She probably reads that magazine, so she probably already knows all that."

Three days later Joey and Gi-Gi came in and ordered boilermakers. They told Kathy they were finished with fancy cocktails forever.

She didn't ask why because she didn't care. She served the

boilermakers, and confessed, "That slow breathing thing helped my insomnia."

"Yeah, well, it didn't do much for Eddie," said Gi-Gi. "He died last night."

"Oh, shit."

The few others at the bar overheard this sad news. After expressions of shock, the place fell silent.

"To Eddie. Watch over Halle, old buddy."

Glasses went up, booze went down.

"What was it?" Kathy asked.

"Basic heart attack. Bing, bang. Here one minute, gone the next."

"But he had a couple other, you know, pre-existing conditions."

Upon reflection and another round, this one on the house, Eddie's friends agreed he caught a break with the heart thing.

95

Free

CHERYL HAD TO pause for a moment with her lawyer. She was technically free but still within prison walls. All she had to do was pass through those doors.

"Are there a lot of them out there?" she asked.

"Yes. You're something of a celebrity now. They'll want a statement."

She wondered if she had the ability to talk to free people under the morning sun.

"Can't you speak for me?"

"They want to hear from you."

She picked at a dry cuticle, a habit she hoped to break.

"I look awful, don't I?"

"You look fine."

"Like, how?"

A woman wants to hear that if she is not beautiful, she is at least attractive in some small way. Cheryl looked like a tweaker but with decent bone structure and hair enough.

She held her lawyer's arm as they stepped into the free world together.

Except for a group of outraged Christians holding signs condemning her to burn in hell and screaming that message at her, it was the kind of gathering most often seen waiting for the release of someone newly found innocent after decades of confinement. Cheryl, however, had admitted to her guilt and had served thirty-one years of a life sentence. She had shot a man in a bar, three times. She was not a hardened violent criminal. Except for that one night. Except for those few minutes one night. Parole boards respond to expressions of remorse and she did not hold back. But none of that mattered much.

With TV cameras trained on her, reporters shouted out the threadbare questions about how she felt. She didn't quite know yet. "What will you do now?" someone asked.

"This isn't over yet," she said in a whiskey bass voice. She wanted to show resilience.

They went to the red meat: "Will you go through with the surgery now, or was that all a clever ploy."

One columnist from the San Francisco Chronicle had been conjecturing in print on whether she would "...give up the lease on the old equipment."

Cheryl had sued the State to provide that surgery, and for a time it looked like they would. It's California. And the court ruled in her favor. When the estimate came in, however, at a little north of one-hundred thousand dollars, the parole board deemed her low-risk and voted to release her. The Governor went along with it.

A woman thrust a microphone into her face and asked, "Would you say you gamed the system, Cheryl?"

"I would say the system gamed me first."

A car pulled up and the lawyer helped her inside.

96

Size Ten and a Half

A FEW WEEKS after Eddie died, Irene told Joey and Gi-Gi to come over and take whatever they wanted. The rest would go to the Catholic Thrift Store.

She emptied his side of the closet and his dresser drawers: socks, mostly white, underwear, always white, T-shirts, two pairs of pajamas, hankies, not much else. He had one good suit, hardly ever worn, an overcoat, a windbreaker, and pants and shirts that he bought for himself on sale, his only criterion for men's wear. Color never mattered to him, price did. He had a Buck pocketknife, a Timex, and some odds and ends. He had a pair of dress shoes, a pair of sneakers, and a pair of desert boots. Those were the ones Irene had stepped into, in her bare feet, for reasons she could not express, when she first sorted out his meager estate.

Nothing takes on the character of the wearer as much as shoes. Unlike shirts and pants, the spirit of the deceased stays in his shoes no matter who wears them going forward. No one thinks about this until faced with the unlaced cavities of a dead man's shoes.

Joey and Gi-Gi embraced Irene and offered again their condolences. They thanked her for giving them first shot at his stuff, which they would respect for the memory. (And they did, toasting him at the bar and saying, "I'm wearing his jacket right now.")

Each of them made a short stack of what they would like to have, no arguments, while Irene sat on the davenport and fought back tears.

"What size shoes do you guys wear?"

Joey said eight and Gi-Gi said ten and a half.

"That was his size, Gi-Gi, go ahead and take the shoes."

Gi-Gi looked at the three pairs as though pondering which one he should take. But he knew he could take none of them.

97

Brucifixion

BRUCIE BUTINSKI, AS his colleagues at the office referred to him, retired to a gated community somewhere in Florida. An obligatory retirement party was thrown after work on his last day. Everyone left early. Those who had long-suffered his skulking and snitching threw their own after-party.

Smith offered a toast. "Free at last!"

Brucie did not consciously set out to be "Florida man…" but buying a gun, a 38-calibre LadySmith, was a good start. He took a shooting course for seniors. He trusted he would be able to handle it well enough if the situation presented itself. It was a fine accessory, and it restored a certain feeling he lost upon retiring.

His only hobby was clipping coupons, and that could be accomplished over morning coffee. He took to walking the circular streets of his gated community as though on patrol, wearing Bermuda shorts and an extra-large Hawaiian shirt to cover the LadySmith holstered on his hip.

On his thrice daily rounds he encountered no suspicious characters or threatening Blacks wearing hoodies, but he did come upon violations of the Design Guideline Booklet, a document he had committed to memory. He noticed as well various failures to keep up with proper maintenance. Whenever that happened, Brucie would ring the offender's doorbell and pleasantly point out the violation. If he had to return and ring the bell again, he was less pleasant, and afterwards would file an official complaint with the HOA board.

His favorite target, or worst offender, depending upon your point-of-view, was Mr. Panino, an elderly widower with two rescue dogs that were mostly chihuahua. Brucie suspected he was hiding a third, which would be a serious violation of HOA rules.

He reported Mr. Panino for the following: improper pruning of his palmetto tree; a doormat of an unapproved color; an uncoiled water hose; a handwritten note to FedEx on his door; and excess wattage on some of his landscape lights.

What Brucie did not know is that although Mr. Panino appeared alone in the world, he was still well-connected back in Cleveland.

One night while Brucie was taking a photo of the corner of an air-conditioning unit that should not have been visible from the street, a car pulled up and he was invited by two large swarthy men to get into the back.

"Who are you and how did you get in here?" Brucie demanded in his most authoritative voice. "This is a private street."

"Shut up and get in the back."

Although armed, Brucie was too frightened to draw his LadySmith, because these men looked like they might have guns, too. He got into the back seat. They drove a short distance to the border of the community, a masonry wall painted pastel yellow. They let him out of the car and took with him the several steps to the wall where one of the men said, "You're gonna lay off Mr. Panino, you little puke."

"You're gonna mind your own business," said the other.

Brucie told them he was *terribly* sorry, and he was sure he would never have occasion to call on Mr. Panino again.

"You got that right."

Brucie spent that night standing against the wall with two spikes hammered through his hands. An organized walking group discovered him in the early morning.

"Florida man crucified in gated community. Claims no memory of the event."

After a short stay in a hospital and a long period of physical therapy, Brucie bought an aquarium full of colorful fish.

98

Same As It Ever Was

STEWART BELIEVED EVERYONE ought to have one thing in his routine he knows to be foolish. For him, it was playing the MegaMillions Lottery twice a week, six dollars a pop. On a good week he'd bet twelve dollars to win three. Still, *somebody* had to win, sooner or later. As the prize grew to dizzying amounts, Stewart got the feeling that this time it would be his turn.

The prize was currently $188,000,000, a figure that spurred the imagination. Here is what he planned to do with his winnings: split it four ways, a share to his wife, a share to each of his children, and a share for himself, to do with as each pleased.

The winner, because of taxes, does not get to keep the whole $188,000,000, but let us say the payout is $100,000,000, after taxes. That was still more money than he could imagine, and as a poet he could imagine everything. The $25,000,000 he would give to each child, cross fingers, would free them from odious labor, though they each seemed satisfied with their jobs. As for him, with $25,000,000 he would never worry about money again. In truth, he never worried much about it before.

As was his habit, he stopped at the Safeway on Wednesday to get his ticket for Friday. The vending machine there was familiar to him, but the process involved several steps, any one of which was possible to screw up, and then you had to start all over again or lament the disappearance of your six dollars. Mistakes occur. Touch the screen to start, feed in your six dollars, touch the MegaMillions icon, agree that there is no turning back, touch the Quick Pick icon, touch the number of chances, three, and finally touch the print icon. Only then does the machine print the ticket and push it through the slot below.

Stewart did all that and reached down for his ticket. He discovered that two tickets were in the slot. He took them both.

He walked to his pickup and weighed the ethical implications. Lotto machines do not make mistakes. What must have happened was that some old coot like him became flummoxed by the process and sacrificed his six dollars because life is too short to rant at a machine. That meant Stewart had his ticket and someone else's. What was the right thing to do? He could go back inside Safeway and try to find the person. Good luck with that. He could give the ticket to the manager, but what would that accomplish? He decided the ticket should stay with him. It meant nothing unless it was a winner. Then Stewart turned his mind to the right thing to do should he win. He could not tell which ticket was his and which was paid for by a person unknown, who surely did his own math on what *he* would do with all that money.

The conundrum was heavy on his mind as he sat and watched the sunset from his deck and sipped his bourbon and petted the old terrier asleep on his lap. The only thing that made moral sense, since he'd already given away $75,000,000 of his winnings to his family, was to give the remaining $25,000,000, his share, to charity. He would spread it across an array of worthy causes.

"I'm probably not going to win anyway," he told the terrier.

Saturday morning, first thing, he checked the newspaper for the winning numbers, the Mega number first, because if you don't hit the Mega you can't hit the jackpot. He did not hit the

Mega number on either ticket. Nor did he hit a single one of the other winning numbers on either of two tickets.

His wife came into the kitchen modeling a new dress she got from Nordstrom's.

"How do I look?" she asked as she spun around.

"Like a million dollars."

99

Blackberry in the Dead of Night

LIGHT IS SOMETHING of a mystery in The Purple Room.

Owen looked up from his notes and noticed five millennials—they travel in packs—at the next table. The sun must have set.

He had come in for Happy Hour. The old crowd was there, but Owen stayed after they left. Drinking Manhattans well into the full price period, he moved from the bar to a table and became lost in ideas, each coming on the heels of the previous one, spreading out in four different directions.

The noses of the millennials were lit up by the phones in their hands, all but one who looked at Owen as though he were an anthropological find.

"'S'up?" asked Owen, in their language.

"I wasn't looking at what you were writing," said the boy.

"Okay."

"But I'm fascinated. You're writing on paper? With a pencil?"

"Are you asking me, or do you not believe your eyes?"

"It's a little odd, though."

"This, BTW., is a moleskin notebook," said Owen, holding it up. "It's what Hemingway favored, though he preferred the small kind. I went through those like M&M's so I switched to the five-by-seven."

"Cool. I guess."

"Indeed."

Owen revealed to the kid that for years he hated Hemingway, because he had wrecked it for everyone else. He wasn't sure the kid knew who Hemingway was, which was okay because he wouldn't have been able to support his own argument anyway.

"I call it my Blackberry," Owen said, and the kid laughed. He would have laughed at a real Blackberry. In his own hands he held the world, updated automatically and frequently. Owen held up his pencil between two fingers like a magic wand. "And this is a Palomino Blackwing Pearl, the prince of pencils, which I am going to have to sharpen soon because it's the soft lead that gives it its character."

"Is that convenient?"

"Convenient? It's essential. It requires me to carry a knife. Not to scare you."

"How do you keep track of your data and access it?"

"This ain't data, and I don't have to keep track of it. I need to read it, again and again, and see where it's going. Data is dead."

"Content, I mean. What if you lose it? Where's your back-up?"

"In here somewhere," said Owen. He tapped the side of his head. "Like The Cloud, only easier to get into. Or it disappears and I have to live with the loss, which is pretty damn humbling."

Owen introduced himself, which is what you do in a bar when you've spent a minute talking to a stranger. The kid told him he was called Dragon Dropp. One of the girls became aware that a conversation was being conducted, for real. She looked up for a second at Owen and then retreated to her e-world.

"I take notes on the phone? With my thumbs?" said the kid, upspeaking. He turned the screen of the phone toward Owen.

"Okay, so I can't even read this. It's a different language. It's just a piece of...content."

"Actually, it's a text."

Owen held his notebook open to the kid.

"Now you read this."

"What is it?"

"A springboard to where you've never been. Don't try too hard to control the landing."

100

Three Miles

DOCIA WENT TO the address on her own without telling Stewart, her brothers or anyone else.

She told her brothers about it later, but by that time their father was dead. They mourned together, not because he died but because for years, he lived only three miles away from where they and their mom moved in with the new husband, a man they would never think of as a dad.

Did her mom know he lived so close? Did they ever run into each other at the market or the post office or a dozen other places they might have?

Her father never made any attempt to see them. That would be—what?—fifth grade through high school and beyond. Childhood illnesses, in Docia's case, a serious one. Little achievements, school plays, football, cheerleading, proms, part-time jobs, drivers' licenses, things that real parents take great joy in seeing.

And then, adulthood, one by one leaving that house, returning to introduce girlfriends and boyfriends, and later with children of their own, until their mother died, and they never had to see their stepfather again. All that time the father who had abandoned them was living only three miles away.

With whom? Doing what?

Docia didn't know.

Her father answered the door wheeling an oxygen tank behind him. He wheezed from the effort. Nothing about him was familiar.

"I think I'm your daughter," she said.

"Do you?"

"I'm Docia."

"How did you find me?"

"Tia Rosa."

"Rosa...could never keep her mouth shut."

"She didn't want to die without telling me."

"It doesn't matter."

"We lived three miles from here." She nodded in that direction. "You could have seen us once in a while."

"Better this way."

"You can tell me. I'm a grown-up now. Explain it a little. I know about a hard life. Mom had to keep us together by picking fruit."

She hoped that she would be invited inside, but all the old man said was, "You should go now."

"Don't you want to know about Roberto and Alfonso?"

The man said nothing.

"They're fine, too. Mom's dead."

"I knew that."

"I don't want anything from you. I only wanted to look at you. And tell you that you have three grandsons and two granddaughters."

"I'm going to shut the door now."

She stopped it with her foot.

"One more thing. We grew up to be decent people with good jobs and loving families. We've never been arrested. Never used drugs. Never joined a gang. We turned out pretty good. You want to know why?"

Her father knew why but did not want to hear it said aloud.

He looked down at Docia's foot blocking the door.

 She stepped back and her father closed the door on her. She could hear the oxygen tank caddy squeak as it rolled away.

Author's Note

The stories *Shaky, Eggshell, Eggshell, Eggshell,* and *Size Ten and a Half* appeared in much different versions in *Andoshen, PA.,* published by Dial Press.

About the Author

Darryl Ponicsán is the author of thirteen novels, including *The Last Detail, Cinderella Liberty, Tom Mix Died for Your Sins* and *An Unmarried Man.*

He's also an award-winning screenwriter for both film and television, with credits including *The Last Detail* (with Jack Nicholson, Otis Young and Randy Quaid), *Cinderella Liberty* (with James Caan and Marsha Mason), *Taps* (with Tom Cruise, Sean Penn and Timothy Hutton), *Vision Quest* (with Matthew Modine, Linda Fiorentino and Madonna), *Nuts* (with Barbra Streisand, Richard Dreyfuss and Leslie Nielsen), *The Boost* (with James Woods and Sean Young), *School Ties* (with Brendan Fraser, Matt Damon and Ben Affleck), *The Enemy Within* (with Forest Whitaker and Dana Delany) and *Random Hearts* (with Harrison Ford and Kristen Scott Thomas).

He recently co-adapted his novel *Last Flag Flying* which serves as a follow-up and spiritual sequel to *The Last Detail* with filmmaker Richard Linklater (*Boyhood* and *Dazed and Confused*), who also directed. The film stars Bryan Cranston, Steve Carell and Laurence Fishburne.

Born in Shenandoah, Pennsylvania, Ponicsán taught high school after attending Muhlenberg College and earning an MA at Cornell University. He served in the US Navy from 1962 to 1965, then did social work in the Watts area of Los Angeles and taught high school before the success of his debut novel, *The Last Detail*, allowed him to become a full-time writer.

He resides in Palm Springs and Sonoma, California.

www.ingramcontent.com/pod-product-compliance
Lightning Source LLC
Chambersburg PA
CBHW030108260626
47156CB00008B/2580